PUFFIN

THE METRO DOGS OF MOSCOW

RACHELLE DELANEY lives in Vancouver, where
she works as a writer, editor, and creative writing teacher. She is the author of *The Ship of Lost
Souls,* which was shortlisted for the Sheila A. Egoff
Children's Literature Prize, the Chocolate Lily
Book Award, and the Red Cedar Book Award, and
two other books in this series. In 2010, Delaney
won the Canadian Authors Association/BookLand
Press Emerging Writer Award. Visit her online at
www.rachelledelaney.com.

Also by Rachelle Delaney

The Lost Souls of Island X

The Ship of Lost Souls

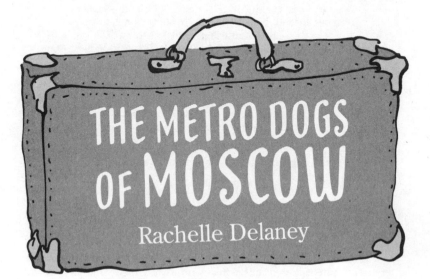

THE METRO DOGS
OF MOSCOW

Rachelle Delaney

PUFFIN

PUFFIN
an imprint of Penguin Canada

Published by the Penguin Group
Penguin Group (Canada), 90 Eglinton Avenue East, Suite 700,
Toronto, Ontario, Canada M4P 2Y3

Penguin Group (USA) Inc., 375 Hudson Street, New York, New York 10014, U.S.A.
Penguin Books Ltd, 80 Strand, London WC2R 0RL, England
Penguin Ireland, 25 St Stephen's Green, Dublin 2, Ireland
(a division of Penguin Books Ltd)
Penguin Group (Australia), 707 Collins Street, Melbourne, Victoria 3008,
Australia (a division of Pearson Australia Group Pty Ltd)
Penguin Books India Pvt Ltd, 11 Community Centre, Panchsheel Park,
New Delhi - 110 017, India
Penguin Group (NZ), 67 Apollo Drive, Rosedale, Auckland 0632, New Zealand
(a division of Pearson New Zealand Ltd)
Penguin Books (South Africa) (Pty) Ltd, 24 Sturdee Avenue, Rosebank,
Johannesburg 2196, South Africa

Penguin Books Ltd, Registered Offices: 80 Strand, London WC2R 0RL, England

First published 2013

5 6 7 8 9 10 (WEB)

Manufactured in Canada.

LIBRARY AND ARCHIVES CANADA CATALOGUING IN PUBLICATION
Delaney, Rachelle
The metro dogs of Moscow / Rachelle Delaney.

ISBN 978-0-14-318414-0

I. Title.

PS8607.E48254M48 2013   jC813'.6   C2012-905939-0

Visit the Penguin Canada website at **www.penguin.ca**
Special and corporate bulk purchase rates available; please see
www.penguin.ca/corporatesales or call 1-800-810-3104, ext. 2477.

ALWAYS LEARNING   PEARSON

For my mom.
Spasibo.

Contents

1
A Very Bad Thing

The key turned in the lock. JR's ears twitched.

Normally, when George arrived home from work, JR would leap out of his bed and skid across the living room to greet him at the door. Today, however, he stayed put.

"What's the matter, boy?" George called, slipping off his shiny leather shoes and carefully lining them up on the top shelf of the closet, where JR couldn't reach them. "You ready for walkies?"

Sometimes JR wished he could speak Human just so he could tell George how ridiculous he sounded when he said "walkies." He buried his nose in his red flannel bed—the one Moira had bought him in Dublin. If he breathed in deeply enough, he could still smell the peat she burned to heat her little weekend cottage by the sea. The thought of Moira made him feel both very sad and slightly better about the Very Bad Thing he'd done while George was at work.

"You sick, boy?" George walked over to JR's spot near the fireplace that wasn't really a fireplace but only looked like one, which was sorely disappointing. He squatted and placed a warm hand on JR's head. George had very soft hands. This was because he worked in an office and moisturized daily. "You don't look sick." JR tried to avoid eye contact and not think about what George would do when he found out. He would yell, that was a given. And he'd probably put JR on biscuit rations. Possibly for life.

"I know what's wrong," said George. "You're still upset about the plane, aren't you?" He paused, as if waiting for JR to agree. "I'm sorry, boy. But there was nothing I could do."

JR had actually forgotten about the plane, but now the memory—awful though it was—made him feel even better about the Very Bad Thing he'd done. There was nothing worse than being forced to travel in the Hold.

This hadn't been the first time he'd had to do it, either. After seven years of moving around, he'd known what was coming when George had announced that they were leaving Dublin for Moscow. Some airlines allowed dogs to travel with their owners in the cabin if they weighed under eight kilograms, which JR, an average-sized Jack Russell terrier, did. The time they'd flown from Helsinki to Kuala Lumpur, he'd been able to sit right on George's lap and charm the flight attendant into giving him extra pretzels. But most airlines had a six-kilogram limit. Any dog that weighed more had to go in the Hold.

During their last few weeks in Dublin, he'd even tried to lose weight, only nibbling at his dinner and valiantly resisting the stray chips and sandwich crusts he came across in St. Stephen's Green, the park they visited every day. But darn George and his pastry habit—how could anyone say no to a daily bite of Danish or croissant? It was George's fault that JR had to travel to Kuala Lumpur in a freezing-cold compartment underneath a thundering plane, his only companions a whiny dachshund and a disgruntled Doberman with bad breath.

Yes, George deserved the Very Bad Thing he had done.

"Look, I'll get changed, and we'll go out exploring, okay?" George said, standing up and shrugging off his pinstriped suit jacket. "We'll go to the park, and maybe find a bakery. I could really go for a croissant." George checked his hair in the mirror over the fireplace, tousling it to make it look like he hadn't spent half an hour styling it that morning. "I wonder if they do croissants in Moscow. Or those buttery things filled with custard we had in Paris. Remember? What were those called?" He wandered off to his bedroom, weaving his way around the piles of boxes he had yet to unpack.

JR held his breath, waiting for the scream. But the only sound from the bedroom was George humming, off-key.

He obviously hadn't looked under the bed.

JR leaped up and raced for the door, grabbing the leash in his mouth on the way. The faster he could get George out of the apartment, the better.

Although they'd lived in Moscow for only five days, JR was fairly certain it would never feel like home. Some parts of their neighbourhood, which George called the Arbat, felt familiar. The old, off-white buildings, for instance, reminded him of their neighbourhood in Paris, which George had called the République. The busy sidewalks, packed with women in high heels and men in shiny leather shoes, felt a bit like Paris, too. And the smell of the mould under the melting snow brought him right back to Helsinki. It was an almost-spring smell that made him want to leap into a mud puddle and have a good roll. George would hate that. Which made him want to do it even more.

But there were new, unfamiliar things in Moscow, too—things he wasn't sure he'd ever feel comfortable with. Like the taxis that came whipping around street corners, sending George sprinting for the sidewalk, his long limbs flailing. And the buildings that butted right up against the sidewalk, without even a sliver of grass between the two. And the sour smell of exhaust that hung in the air, sometimes so thick that JR could barely discern the almost-spring smells of mud and snow mould. He'd lived in plenty of cities, but never had he lived in a city quite so *cityish.*

Their apartments, however, were always the same: small, plain, and on the first floor, since heights made George nervous. They came furnished with a bed, tables, couch, and desk, for as George always said, "Globetrotting George can't own furniture. It would only weigh him down."

Sometimes JR wished he could find the bonehead who came up with the name "Globetrotting George" and give him a good, hard bite on the ankle.

He tugged George out the front lobby and into the mild afternoon. The flat, off-white sky matched the flat, off-white buildings perfectly. Hopefully, the park would be more interesting. Maybe there would be something small and furry or feathered to chase. Or better yet, something squeaky. He picked up the pace.

"Hey, slow down, boy! What's the hurry?" George tugged on the leash, but JR ignored him. His paws were itching for a run on the grass. If only George would let him off-leash, like he used to at Moira's cottage. JR would race along the beach, chasing seagulls or sandpipers or nothing at all, his tongue flapping in the salty air.

But George never let him off-leash in the city. He seemed to think that if JR spotted something small and squeaky, he'd take off after it and never look back. Which was true. But it still didn't seem fair.

They turned right at the corner, passed another row of off-white apartments, then hung a left at the corner store that smelled like cigarettes and sausages. Its window was stacked with bottles of water and rolls of toilet paper, and judging by a whiff that tickled JR's nostrils, there were some half-stale loaves of rye bread in there, too.

A bearded man—probably the owner—was standing at the door, arms folded over his big, round belly, watching people pass. George nodded politely and offered a *"Dobryj utro,"* one of the only phrases in Russian he knew. It meant "Good morning."

The store owner raised an eyebrow and looked purposefully at his watch. George didn't notice.

"Maybe we'll find a bakery down this way," he said, turning toward a street they hadn't yet explored.

But just as JR was turning to look, something caught his eye. Something dark and shadowy, moving in the narrow space between the corner store and the building next to it. He ground to a halt.

"Aw, c'mon, boy." George tugged on the leash. "You want a pastry, don't you? Something chocolatey? Oh wait, you can't eat chocolate. Maybe something—"

JR ignored him again, staring at the spot where he'd seen something move, until sure enough, the shadow slipped out into the light.

It was a dog. A big dog, nearly three times as tall as JR and possibly twice as old. He had matted brown hair, mud-caked paws, and a nasty scar over his right eye. And he definitely needed a good bath; even where JR stood, about twenty feet away, the smell made him wince. It was like George's gym shoes stuffed with that awful blue cheese he liked so much. It also made him suddenly thankful for the cramped, boring apartment they'd just left. At least he had a place to live. This dog obviously didn't.

Then the dog turned toward him and gave him the oddest look. It took JR a moment to realize that it was a look of *pity*—probably the same look JR had been giving him. This dog—this homeless, dirty dog—felt sorry for him!

But why? Naturally, JR was smaller, but probably just as fast. And sure, he had a human who said stupid things like "walkies" and moisturized far more often than necessary, but at least he *had* a human. So what was there to pity? What did this stray have that he didn't?

Suddenly, the store owner started hollering and waving his arms. The stray looked over at him, and when he looked back at JR, the look of pity had disappeared, replaced by one of mischief—a look that said, "Watch *this*!" And he took off. But instead of running away from the store owner, he ran straight for him! As JR and George watched, open-mouthed, the stray ducked between the owner's legs and ran right into the shop, emerging moments later with an entire sausage ring in his mouth. He raced off, the hollering owner hot on his heels, but not before giving JR one last look—a look that said clearly, "Bet you wish you could do *that*!"

Never had JR wanted anything more.

"Wow. Didja see that, boy? Sneaky thing. I think he was a stray," George remarked as he watched the owner and dog disappear around a corner. "I hear there's a lot of them in Moscow. We'll have to watch out. Wouldn't want you getting rabies or anything." He leaned down and stroked JR's head. "But don't worry. I'll always keep you on the leash."

JR closed his eyes and forced himself not to bite George's well-moisturized hand. It made him feel *much* better about the Very Bad Thing awaiting George back at home.

2
Walkies

JR wasn't sure what this new park was called. When they'd first happened upon it, days ago, George had stopped and stared at the name on the sign. After a long while, he'd nodded sagely, concluding, "The Russians use an entirely different alphabet, boy."

Whatever its name was, it had nothing on St. Stephen's Green. St. Stephen's was lush and leafy and dotted with ponds full of plump, jabbering ducks. This park had three skinny, leafless trees and not a pond in sight—just a wide gravel path that wound around a few pitiful patches of brown grass. Fifty such parks could have fit inside St. Stephen's Green, with room to spare.

Today, some other dogs were doing their business on the patches of brown grass. Embassy dogs, JR guessed, for two reasons. First, there were a lot of embassy workers in the Arbat neighbourhood. And second, the dogs were all on-leash. JR had long suspected it was the leash that made embassy dogs, like the neighbourhoods they lived in, so very boring.

He pictured the stray, who'd probably never known a leash in his life, and his paws started to feel twitchy. It was the kind of twitchiness he felt before he did something Very Bad. He swallowed hard. Very Bad Things always happened very fast— so fast he couldn't stop them even if he wanted to. One second he'd be doing something innocent, like counting ceiling tiles, and the next second he'd be mauling the coffee table. He tried hard to concentrate on the park before him.

One of the humans—a blond man with broad shoulders—waved at George. He held the leashes of two medium-sized dogs with long grey and white hair, blue eyes, and speckled snouts. Australian shepherds, JR knew. He'd met one once in Helsinki.

George smoothed some wrinkles in his sweater. "That's the Australian Ambassador to Russia, boy," he whispered. "He lives two buildings down from us." George himself worked for the Canadian Embassy, but he was nowhere near as important as an ambassador. Mostly, he ran around and fetched things for more important people.

"Hello, Mr. Cowley," George greeted the big blond man, a little nervously. "I'm George Cooper. We met at the corner store the other day."

JR paused a few feet away from the Australian shepherds, sizing them up. The shepherd in Helsinki had been friendly, but you could never be too careful.

The man nodded. "Of course. You're the new Canadian. Call me John." He gripped George's hand and shook it, hard. JR could tell George was holding back a whimper.

"Hullo." One of the shepherds ambled right up to JR and flopped onto the ground in front of him. It was a submissive gesture, and one that JR, at a foot tall, rarely received. "I'm Pie. What's your name?"

"Pie?" JR repeated. "Like pumpkin pie?"

"Or apple," Pie said agreeably. "Or lemon meringue." He flipped over onto his side and looked up at JR with a pleasantly blank expression.

"He's not choosy," the other shepherd said, giving JR a sniff but not lowering himself to the ground. "I'm Robert, his brother. Pie, get up. You've made your point." Robert obviously wasn't the submissive type.

Not for the first time, JR was grateful for the fact that no matter where George dragged him in the world, dogs seemed to speak the same language. Even when George couldn't converse with their owners, JR could speak to the dogs.

"I'm JR," he told them.

Robert chuckled. "For Jack Russell."

"Uh-huh." JR nodded, wishing for about the hundredth time that George had spent a bit more time coming up with his name. George was a lot of things, but creative wasn't one of them. His idea of art was using his computer to draw moustaches and bow ties on the people in his photos.

It took Pie a few moments to figure it out. Finally, he sat up. "Oh, I get it! JR. Jack Russell. Robert, how did you figure that out so fast?"

Robert winked at JR. "New to the 'hood, are ya? We've only been here a month ourselves. Lived in London for three years before this. You?"

"Dublin," said JR. "Paris before that. And Kuala Lumpur and Helsinki before Paris."

Robert gave a low whistle. "Sounds exciting."

Pie nodded politely, but judging by the look in his eyes, he thought it sounded rather terrifying. Pie would obviously not do well in the Hold.

"It used to be," JR admitted. "But now, well, I'd take a real home over globetrotting any day."

There, he'd said it. And it felt good to finally tell someone, since he obviously couldn't tell the Globetrotter himself. He looked up at George, who for some reason was telling John Cowley about the spiders in their Kuala Lumpur apartment. George felt the same way about spiders as he did about heights.

"I hear ya," Robert said. "We were gutted to leave our flat in London. Lived right near Hyde Park."

"Did you get to go off-leash?" JR asked.

"Nah," said Robert. "Old John thinks we might get swiped by dognappers." He chuckled. "I'd love to go off-leash, but it'll never happen on his watch."

"I don't know." Pie chewed on a toenail. "I kind of like the leash."

JR sniffed a toothpick someone had dropped on the grass. This was exactly what was wrong with embassy dogs. They travelled the world but never *saw* anything. Never explored or had adventures. And like Pie, most of them were just fine with that.

"How 'bout you?" Robert asked. "Your owner let you off?"

"Never in the city," said JR. "But he had a girl-friend in Dublin with a cottage by the sea, and he'd let me off when we went there."

That was all it took for the memories to come flooding back. All at once, JR was back in County Clare, running along the cliffs and rolling in moss or heather or anything that smelled intriguing. Later, he'd collapse in his red flannel bed in front of the peat fire and fall asleep to the rise and fall of George and Moira's voices and the distant crash of waves on the cliffs. It was the most fun he'd ever had, not to mention the closest he'd ever come to having a real home.

He was about to tell Robert and Pie all about it when a new dog trotted over. She was grey and

black and not so much big as extremely fluffy—
obviously groomed daily. She had a dainty, cat-like
face made more cat-like by the prim look she was
giving them.

"Hullo, Beatrix." Pie immediately dropped to
the ground at her spotless paws.

Robert sighed at his brother. "Hey, Beatrix.
This is JR. He's new to the 'hood. JR, Beatrix. She's
from the Netherlands. Ever been?"

JR shook his head. But knowing George, it was
only a matter of time.

"You should," Beatrix informed him. "It's a
very forward-thinking country."

"Oh." JR wasn't sure what it meant to be
forward-thinking, but he didn't particularly want
to hear Beatrix explain it.

"You're a Jack Russell," she observed, tossing
her well-groomed head.

"Uh-huh. And you're ...?" He had never seen a
dog quite so ... fluffy.

"A keeshond," Beatrix said. "That's *kays*-hond,
not *kees*-hond, like some dogs think." She shot
Robert a reproachful look and lifted a small paw
to smooth her whiskers. Robert winked at JR again.

"My human is Johanna Van Wingerden."
Beatrix nodded at the woman holding her leash,
who was shaking hands with George. "She's very
high up in the Dutch Embassy."

Johanna Van Wingerden, looking just as prim as Beatrix, was dressed in a navy suit and high heels that were slowly sinking into the mud. Her hair was pulled back in a tight knot, and she smelled like hairspray and Earl Grey tea. "And where are you from?" Beatrix asked.

"Canada," JR said. "A city called Ottawa." It had been seven years since he'd lived there (human years, of course; more like forty in dog years), but he could still remember the barn he and his brothers had been born in, on a farm outside the city. It had smelled sweet like hay and tangy like leather, and the tall, rustly grasses around it were full of squeaky things to chase.

That was about the extent of his memories, but it was enough to convince him that Ottawa was paradise. Unfortunately, George didn't agree. Home seemed to be the one place where he didn't care to live.

"JR was just telling us about his travels," Robert told Beatrix. "He's been all over."

JR looked back up at George. He was talking about the spiders again, gesturing with his hands to show John and Johanna how big they were (about three times the size they actually were). Normally, JR didn't like to complain, especially about George. Embassy dogs almost never complained about their humans—except for the dachshunds, but they complained about everything.

But today, well, today was different. Today, he was twitchy. He'd already done one Very Bad Thing, and if he didn't let out his frustrations, who knew what he'd do next?

He took a deep breath. "George is a globetrotter," he began. "At least, he thinks he is. But I know better. I know he wants a real home as much as I do."

Robert smacked his lips. "A classic case of dog knowing human better than human knows himself. We know that well, don't we, Pie?"

"Mm-hmm," Pie agreed, looking fondly up at John. "John only *thinks* he doesn't like it when I eat the mail before he can open it. But I know he must like it, because then he doesn't see his bills."

Beatrix stared at Pie for a moment, then shook her head. She turned back to JR. "I've heard Johanna say that most embassy workers stay in one place for a few years at least. So why does your human keep moving?"

"It started about eight years ago," said JR. "This was before I was born, but George has told me all about it. A *lot*. He never seems to realize that he's telling me the same stories over and over again."

"They never do," Beatrix said knowingly.

"He was working as a waiter back in Ottawa. At the Cheesecake Café," he went on.

"Mmm. Cheesecake," Pie said, and Robert shushed him. "Sorry," he whispered, and went back to chewing on his toenail.

"One night after work, he started telling his waiter friends about his dream to see the world. And one of them suggested he work for the Canadian Embassy abroad. George hadn't actually meant that he wanted to *live* someplace else, but his friends started calling him Globetrotting George, and he didn't want to let them down."

"Typical pack mentality," Beatrix commented. Robert shushed her, too, and she glared back.

"So he applied," said JR, "and eventually he was offered a job at the embassy in Finland. That was only because they couldn't find anyone else who spoke Finnish, and George had learned it in high school to impress a girl." George did a lot of things to impress girls. Like wearing cologne that smelled like an old fishing boat (although JR had his doubts that this actually worked).

"That's when he decided to get me. He wanted a companion to take with him, but not one that would complain about moving all the time."

Beatrix tsked. Robert gave George's pant leg a disdainful look, as if considering doing his business on it.

"But here's the worst part," JR continued, encouraged. "It never fails. We'll move to a place and start to explore, and at first it's an adventure—there's all kinds of new things to eat and smell. Then George finds a girlfriend—he always does—and the three of us will start having dinners together, and going for walks and weekend trips. And for a while, it's all good. But then, just as we're settling in, just as it's starting to feel like we've got a home, he goes and does it."

"What?" Pie looked up from his toenail.

"He says we have to move. He says, 'We're rolling stones, JR. We can gather no moss.'"

"What does that mean?" Pie whispered to Robert, who shrugged.

"I don't know either," said JR. "But I know it has to do with his friends back home, who call him Globetrotting George. They say, 'You're living the dream, George,' and he feels like he has to. He can't settle down with anyone because it'd mean he'd have to stay in one place."

"Commitment issues," Beatrix remarked.

"So he convinces the embassy that he needs a transfer, and I don't know why, but they always manage to find him something," JR concluded. He paused to catch his breath, suddenly aware that he was sounding very whiny, possibly dachshund-like. But now his head was swirling with pictures of everything and everyone they'd left behind. Like Tiia in Helsinki, who had the tastiest purple sneakers. And Sophie in Paris, who worked at a bakery and hid biscuits for JR in her apron pockets. And Moira, who'd probably already found someone to replace George—someone with a dog to run off-leash at her cottage by the sea. JR gulped. What if it was a dachshund? Or worse, a Pomeranian!

He chewed hard on his lip. He was sick of it. Sick of the moving, the Hold, the tiny apartments, the dogs at the park who were destined to stay tethered to their humans forever. He was sick and tired of being one of them.

"Easy there, J." Robert pushed his nose gently into JR's shoulder. "You look like you're going to shred something."

JR shook his head. Robert had no idea how right he was.

But Beatrix did. She narrowed her eyes at him. "You already did, didn't you?"

"What? Shred something?" JR swallowed hard, picturing what lay under George's bed. "No."

"You did," she said flatly. "Was it something important?"

"No!" he insisted. But she wouldn't look away. He sighed. "Okay, yes."

Robert's eyes lit up, and he leaned in closer. "Something expensive?"

"Maybe." JR scratched at the grass, wishing they'd all just go away.

"I do that all the time," said Pie.

"He does," Robert agreed. "Last time John went away on business, Pie shredded the whole carpet. By the time John got home, it was a pile of string."

"He didn't like that much," Pie recalled. "At least, he didn't *think* he liked it. But *I* think he did, because then he didn't have to vacuum."

Beatrix stared at Pie, then shook her head again. "That's very bad manners."

JR looked up at George, hoping he might get the hint and take him home before the embassy dogs could ask exactly what he'd destroyed. But fortunately, Johanna Van Wingerden provided a distraction.

"Ugh!" she exclaimed, winding Beatrix's leash tighter around her wrist. "I saw one the other day too! Filthy thing. I hear there's rabies everywhere in Moscow."

"We saw a stray," Beatrix explained. "Just down the street from our apartment. She had fleas, I could just tell." She shuddered.

"Well, I doubt there's rabies *everywhere*, but—" John began.

"Everywhere!" Johanna cut in, pulling her high heel out of the grass and then stomping it back in, deeper. "We can never be too careful! Never take your dog off-leash!"

Robert groaned. "Great, now she's done it."

"Johanna's right," Beatrix said, moving closer to her human's leg. "We can't be too careful. Besides, it's not as if your human lets you off-leash anyway."

JR gritted his teeth, trying not to think about how it had felt to be off-leash in Ireland.

"Have you guys seen much of Moscow?" he asked, although he knew what their answer would be.

The dogs all shook their heads.

"Never been more than a few blocks from home," said Robert. "But John says it's interesting. The other day, he went to the Gremlin—"

"Kremlin," Beatrix corrected him.

"Yeah, that," said Robert. "And he saw some guy who'd been dead for, like, eighty years, lying in a dark room, all preserved as if he'd just died yesterday."

"They call him Lenin," Beatrix informed them.

"I call him spooky," said Robert. "But I wouldn't mind seeing the Gremlin. That's what I'd do if I could go off-leash."

Pie shivered. "I'd be afraid of getting lost," he whispered to his toenail.

JR thought of the stray, who didn't seem the type to get lost. He probably knew Moscow like the back of his paw.

In fact, he mused as they headed back to the apartment, it was possible that that homeless dog felt more at home than JR ever had.

3
Escape

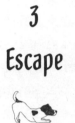

Inga, the cleaning lady, had been by while they were out. Not that there was much for her to clean—everything except JR's bed and George's three most prized possessions was still in boxes. This was another maddening thing about George: he'd move them across the world in mere days, but it took him ages to unpack.

The only thing that would eventually force him to empty out the boxes was meeting a girl he liked. He'd invite her over to show off his cooking skills, and half an hour before she arrived, he'd sprint around the apartment, tossing books on the shelves and lining up suits in the closet. He'd stuff the kitchen cupboards with spices, garlic, and canned tomatoes, turn on some jazz on the stereo, and start sautéing onions for soup. And finally, the apartment would start to feel like home.

And humans thought dogs were predictable.

Still, Inga came every other day to search for any white and brown dog hairs that had escaped the dustpan on her last visit. JR didn't mind her. She had soft grey eyes and calloused fingers that went straight for the sweet spot behind his left ear. She'd chat to him as she cleaned, and although he didn't have a clue what she was saying, it sounded pleasant enough—probably something about how well her grandchildren did on their spelling tests. She also didn't move his bed from its place near the fireplace that wasn't really a fireplace. Which was nice.

"Chilly in here," George commented as they came through the door. "Inga must've left the window open."

If JR could have spoken Human, he would have informed George that she did it every time, to get rid of the smell of his cologne.

The cologne collection was one of the prized possessions George had actually bothered to unpack. He had three scents: "Cowboy" (leather and a hint of cinnamon, for evenings out), "Hero" (jasmine and lemongrass, for days at the office), and "Sailor" (old fishing boat, for weekend adventures that never involved sailing because George was afraid of deep water).

His second prized possession was the T.K. Wanderer Silverback Shaving Brush. He'd bought it in Helsinki for a price that would have kept JR in dry food for the rest of his life.

"It's completely worth it, boy!" George had insisted. "It's the *crème de la crème* of shaving brushes. Made with real badger hair!"

JR had never known a badger, but he didn't imagine they deserved to be used to paint human faces with shaving cream. The sight of the T.K. Wanderer Silverback still made him queasy.

And then there was George's third prized possession. Which now lay under the bed in several dozen pieces.

"Ready for a snack, boy?" George called, heading for the couch with the box of pastries he'd bought on the way home. "I can't wait to try some Russian goodies." He set his box on the coffee table and pulled out what appeared to be a fried dumpling filled with spiced apples. "They called this a *piroshki*. Looks good, huh?"

He unfolded the English newspaper he always picked up at work and proceeded to devour his pastry while catching up on the news. JR headed for his flannel bed by the fireplace that wasn't really a fireplace to wait for George to toss him a piece of *piroshki*.

"Looks like the Russians won the hockey championships again," George commented over a mouthful of fried dough and apples. It sounded more like "Wooks wike da Wussians won da hockey chummions again."

JR stared hard at George's snack, waiting for him to remember his manners.

He didn't. "One of the metro lines was down yesterday, so everyone trying to get to work got stranded," George reported, licking bits of apple off his wrist. "Glad I can walk to work. John has to take the metro every day, since the Australian Embassy's way across town, and he says it's just chaos. Thousands of people rushing off to work, elbowing and pushing each other for a spot on the train." George shook his head. "No thank you."

JR's belly growled. He sighed loudly, but George didn't notice.

The phone in George's pocket buzzed, and he pulled it out to see who was calling. Then, before JR could object, he gulped down the last of his *piroshki* and ran his tongue along his teeth.

Humans. JR sank down into his bed and buried his nose in flannel.

"Hello? Oh, hey, Conrad. Tonight? Oh, well, okay. Sure, sounds good. I'll meet you there."

George hung up and shrugged. "Looks like I'm going out, boy. Conrad—he's the Canadian ambassador's executive assistant—wants to check out some art exhibit. I guess there's a famous artist who sets up surprise exhibits in public places, and everyone rushes out to see them. His name's Phil or something."

He stood and yawned. "I'd kind of rather stay and hang out. That reality show about the figure skaters is on tonight."

JR sighed again. Why anyone would want to watch a reality show about figure skaters—especially in a language they didn't understand—was beyond him.

"But at least this'll be a good chance to meet people," George continued. Of course, by "people" he meant "girls."

George headed for the bedroom, and once again, JR braced himself for the scream. But nothing happened. George emerged ten minutes later in a dress shirt and jeans, smelling like leather and a hint of cinnamon.

"I can't find my watch," he said, pulling his pockets inside out. "You haven't seen it, have you, boy?"

JR sank deeper into his bed.

"Maybe I left it at work." George checked his hair in the mirror. "I sure hope so. I'd be lost without the Dumont-Sauvage Seafaring Nomad AC III."

JR closed his eyes, remembering the Dumont-Sauvage Seafaring Nomad AC III in happier times, when it was still waterproof to up to a thousand feet (not that it mattered, with George's fear of deep water) and indestructible at zero gravity (another feature wasted, with his fear of heights).

"The hands are studded with rocks from a meteorite, boy!" George had exclaimed when he'd brought it home from a shop in Paris, after saving for an entire year to buy it. It was his third prized possession.

And now it was a mound of mechanical parts under his bed.

"I think I'll be out late, boy!" George called as he pulled on his shoes. "Don't wait up!" And he slipped out the door, without even tossing JR a goodbye biscuit.

JR sat in his bed for a while, mulling it all over. Part of him was relieved that George still hadn't discovered the pile of shiny parts that used to be his watch. Another part of him was still put out that George hadn't bothered to share his *piroshki*. But mostly, he just felt empty. Not hungry-empty; there was dry food in his dish near the door, and by the smell of it, some sticky crumbs on the couch where George had been sitting. No, this was a different kind of empty. The emptiness that came with knowing he had an entire evening to kill in a boring apartment, in a city he'd never know.

And with that emptiness came the twitchiness, back with a vengeance.

He closed his eyes and tried to think of something, *anything,* to distract himself from doing another Very Bad Thing. But all he could think of was the muddy, matted stray racing down the street with a ring of sausage in his mouth and a look of pure joy in his eyes.

JR began to salivate. He opened his eyes and blinked hard.

That's when he saw the window—the one Inga had left open. Its curtains were trembling in the breeze.

She hadn't left it open wide, just six inches or so.

Just wide enough for an average-sized Jack Russell terrier to slip through.

It happened like it always did when twitchiness was involved. One second he was sitting in bed, watching the curtains shiver, and the next thing he knew, his paws were hitting the cold concrete a few feet below the window.

He paused only a second to consider what he'd done before racing off down the street, his tongue flapping in the almost-spring air.

4

Moscow

Never—not at the farm where he was born, or even at Moira's cottage by the sea—had JR felt so free. He sprinted straight down the sidewalk, dodging several pairs of legs, then hung a sharp right at the corner and zoomed up the next street. The wind rushed deep into his ears, and he opened his mouth wide so that the smell and taste of dirt and pavement could flow right through him.

After a few minutes, though, he realized that if he ever wanted to find his way home, he had better pay attention to where he was going. He slowed to a jog and looked around. There was the corner store they'd passed on the way to the park, except now it was dark, locked up for the night.

The sun was setting behind the buildings, giving them a soft, purple glow—much nicer than their usual off-white. Somewhere, someone was practising the flute, and across the street, the lights were coming on in an apartment building. In one window, a young boy set the dinner table while his older sister supervised. In another, a woman collapsed in an armchair and grimaced as she tugged off her tall black boots.

This was much, much better than those figure skaters he'd be watching if George had stayed home. And to think he'd almost missed this! Good old Conrad, the executive assistant. And good old Phil, the mysterious artist.

JR was so taken by the window scenes that he didn't notice the couple strolling toward him until they were almost on top of him. Then he jumped out of the way, squishing himself up against the nearest building before they could—well, who knew what Muscovites did with dogs they found off-leash? But the couple just strolled on past, she in a long fur coat and he in a black suit jacket. Neither gave him so much as a glance.

He watched them go, remembering what George had said about all the stray dogs in Moscow. Could there really be so many that people barely noticed them?

Which brought up another question: had the couple actually thought JR was a stray? He wrinkled his nose, picturing the stinky dog at the corner store. Surely these people knew a civilized dog—a *purebred*—when they saw one.

He took another deep breath of evening air, choked a bit on the gasoline fumes, then set off in the same direction the stray had taken. He had no idea where the street would lead, and that in itself felt wonderful. He was an explorer. An adventurer. A *real* globetrotter.

His hind legs did a little dance.

Soon, more and more people were joining him on the sidewalk. Some pulled squeaky grocery carts while others tapped messages into their phones as they walked. Three teenagers ran by, shouting, and an old woman in a head scarf shook her fist at them. But no one seemed to take any notice of JR.

He looked down at his paws, wondering if maybe he wasn't really there at all. Maybe it was all a dream, and he was actually home in bed.

But then, he was hit with a waft of something powerful—something so delicious that he knew he couldn't be dreaming. Some mix of tomatoes and garlic and … He sniffed and concentrated. Pork. A sweet, smoky pork stew. The fumes were drifting over from a nearby restaurant.

JR went to the window and pressed his nose up against it. Inside, humans hunched over bowls of steaming stew and plates of crispy lamb kebabs.

He was watching so intently that, once again, he didn't notice the approaching human until he was standing right beside him. It was a server from the restaurant, out to wipe down the glass menu case. JR held his breath, bracing for the man to yell at him to get away. But the server simply cleaned the case and then went back inside without even looking at JR.

Stunned, he turned and walked away. Maybe ... he mused. Maybe Moscow wasn't so bad after all. Maybe it was a place where humans and canines lived side by side in an equal, respectful partnership. A place where dogs could wander free and unleashed. A place where—

"Sobaka!"

He looked up to see a tall, skinny man in sunglasses and a black hat walking toward him, holding a cardboard box in one hand. A cardboard box that smelled like potatoes, cheese, and ... JR sniffed and concentrated again. *Bacon.*

Handouts? JR stopped, unable to believe his luck. Moscow truly was amazing!

"Sobaka!" the man said again, stopping right in front of JR and bending over, holding out his empty hand. JR looked from the man's hand to his face. There was something unsettling about not being able to see a human's eyes. You could tell so much just by looking into them.

But before JR could take a step back and study him, the man reached out, grabbed him by the scruff of his neck, and lifted him several feet off the ground.

JR squealed and squirmed, but the man held fast. He smelled like onions and paint thinner—a smell so powerful that even the thing in the box, which seemed to be a stuffed potato, couldn't overpower it. JR felt faint.

Then the man began muttering something— quite possibly about how he was going to make JR into a shaving brush. He held him up higher and turned him around, inspecting him for who knew what horrible purpose. A passing couple stepped out of the way, eyeing the man warily but not bothering to rescue JR. He whimpered and squirmed again, but the man wouldn't let go. Instead, he cocked his head to the side, then nodded, satisfied about something.

This was it, then. This was how it was all going to end—on the streets of Moscow, which, as it turned out, wasn't a nice place after all. George would feel just terrible. He'd probably bronze JR's leash. But who would eat the new box of treats in the hall closet? Would George bring them to the dog park for those embassy dogs to devour? Would he—

Just then, the man let out a piercing scream, followed by what even JR could tell were some nasty Russian curse words. And before he knew what was happening, the man had let him go, and he was falling to the ground.

It all seemed to happen in slow motion. The ground was moving toward him, or maybe he toward it. Either way, it was going to be painful. And something was falling alongside him. Something that smelled like ... bacon. The box! He watched it open as it fell, releasing a potato wrapped in foil. It glinted in the headlights of a passing car.

But *then,* something was leaping *up!* Something big and golden, grabbing the potato in mid-air! It was ... it was ...

At this point, JR hit the pavement. There was a thud, and for a few moments, everything went black.

When he opened his eyes, time was back to normal. Unfortunately, nothing else was. The skinny man was still standing above him, yelling, but now there were two, no, *three* other dogs swarming around his legs. One—tall, sleek, and golden—had the potato clamped between her teeth, and the other two were making sure the man didn't touch her.

There wasn't a leash in sight, which could only mean one thing.

They were all strays.

"Let's go!" yelled a lanky male with short hair that was probably reddish-brown underneath all the dirt. He turned tail and ran, and the golden dog followed with the potato. JR was just debating whether he ought to go, too, when once again he was lifted up by the scruff of his neck. Except this time by teeth.

"Come on, son." A dog he couldn't see set him down, then gave him a shove, propelling him after the others. "Time to go!"

He didn't argue, didn't even turn around. Off he scampered, weaving in and out of human legs, dodging grocery carts and baby strollers, trying to keep his eyes on the golden dog loping away on her long, long legs.

"Into the alley!" the dog behind him barked. "On your right!"

JR veered into a dark, narrow space between two buildings. Only when he was already deep inside it did he pause to consider whether following a pack of strays into a dark alley was really a good idea.

"Are you all right, son?" His rescuer drew up beside him.

Finally, JR turned to look at him. It was an older dog, brown and dirty with matted fur and—

The stray from the corner store! Up close, his face was criss-crossed with scars, including the nasty one over his right eye.

"Oh, yeah. Yeah, I'm fine," JR said, trying not to stare. "Um, thanks … for the rescue."

The old dog chuckled. "I think Ania was actually going for the Kroshka Kartoshka."

"Who? What?"

He nodded toward the potato, which the other two were in the midst of devouring. "Kroshka Kartoshka. The street food of the gods. Except now it's the food of the street dogs!" He grinned at his own joke and smacked his lips. "I'd usually partake, but I'm still full from those sausages." He winked at JR.

"Oh. Right." So he *did* remember him! JR wasn't sure what else to say. He looked around the alley, at the piles of rotting garbage and puddles of cloudy water underfoot. Then he pictured his apartment. He could be sleeping by the fireplace that wasn't really a fireplace right now, but instead, he was in a filthy alley with strays that probably had fleas, and quite possibly rabies. He was starting to feel sick.

The golden dog swallowed the last of her share of the stuffed potato, then shook herself hard. Without even glancing at JR, she trotted back to the entrance of the alley and peered out. Moments later she returned, shaking her head. She had furry gold ears that stood straight up, a long, narrow snout, and almond-shaped eyes.

As an average-sized Jack Russell terrier, JR was used to feeling intimidated by other dogs, although he tried never to let himself sink to the ground like Pie had. But this one—Ania, his rescuer had called her—was different. She didn't make him want to sink to the ground, but she did make it difficult for him to stop staring at her.

Still, he forced himself to say something. "Thanks," he offered, then cleared his throat and tried again. "Um ... I owe you." Which was a ridiculous thing to say. What could he possibly do for her?

Finally, she turned to look at him. Her eyes were grey, like the sky over Dublin in November. He stared down at a murky puddle to stop himself from staring.

After a long moment, she said, "You're welcome. You all right?"

JR nodded, hoping she hadn't heard him whimpering.

"I think some introductions are in order," said the brown dog. "I am Boris, and this is Ania. And that stomach on legs is Fyodor." He waited for Fyodor to glance up from his meal, but he didn't. Boris sighed. "Kids these days. No manners. And you are?"

"JR," said JR.

Finally, Fyodor looked up, burped, and wandered over. He was a few inches shorter than Ania, skinny and small-eyed. He stopped beside JR to sniff him thoroughly, and JR willed himself to stay upright. This was no time to pull a Pie.

"Not from around here, obviously," Fyodor observed. "Where you from? The suburbs?"

"No," said JR, trying to stop the tremor in his left hind leg. "I'm ... I'm with the Canadian Embassy."

As soon as it was out of his mouth, he knew it was the wrong thing to say.

Sure enough, Fyodor hooted. "The embassy! Well, we're honoured, Your Majesty." He bowed, then turned away. "Come on, Ania. Let's get back to business." He didn't say "without this guy," but it was obvious he meant it.

"Fyodor," Boris said sharply. "Mind your manners." He turned to JR. "Why are you out by yourself, son? Where's your human?"

JR shrugged, looking away from Fyodor's jeer. "I just ... wanted to see the city. I wanted to explore."

"You did!" Boris's eyes lit up. "Ania, did you hear that? He wants to see the city!"

"That's nice," Ania replied, looking back at the entrance to the alley.

"That is excellent," Boris told JR. "Embassy dogs rarely care to see the city. We met one once—a chihuahua from the Mexican Embassy. Remember, Ania? What was his name? Juan?"

"Jorge, I think," Ania said, still looking away.

"Anyway, he wanted nothing to do with Moscow. Never even gave it a chance. But you, well, if you want to see the city, then we will show it to you!"

Fyodor groaned. "C'mon, Boris," he said. "We don't want him tagging along. He's … he's …" He lowered his voice. "One of them."

JR cringed, wanting to protest, to tell them that he wasn't like the other embassy dogs—or at least, he didn't want to be. But he stayed quiet, knowing they wouldn't believe him anyway.

Boris shook his head. "You need to learn to be a good ambassador."

"Ania, what do you say?" Fyodor turned to her. "Do we get back to business? Or do we spend our night taking Embassy here on a tour?"

"And doing our duty as Muscovites," Boris added, also turning to Ania.

She tore her eyes away from the alley entrance, settling them on JR once more. She looked him up and down and back up again, and he drew himself up as tall as he could. Finally, she shrugged. "I don't see why we can't do both. Do you?" She turned to Fyodor, who opened his mouth to argue, then seemed to think better of it and snapped it shut.

Ania turned back to JR. "Think you can keep up?"

He glanced quickly at Fyodor, who curled his lip, then at Boris, who nodded encouragingly. He gulped and nodded.

"Then we'll give you the Grand Tour," said Ania.

5

Kroshka Kartoshka

Keeping up was easier said than done. Only five minutes after they left the alley, JR was already winded from weaving in and out of crowds, hopping on and off sidewalks, and darting across busy streets. He was panting hard, quickly falling behind, and cursing George's leisurely walkies for making him so out of shape.

Ania led them down a ramp into an underground passage, which appeared to be a way for humans to cross a busy intersection without having to stop for traffic. It was a maze of dim hallways lined with shops selling cigarettes, scarves, and pastries. JR wondered if George knew about these underground pastry shops. Maybe he stopped in here on his way to work.

"Left up ahead," Boris called. He had insisted that, as the official tour guide, he'd take up the rear, but JR was fairly certain he was just making sure the embassy dog didn't get lost. Which was nice of him, but embarrassing, too.

If only George had made fewer pastry runs. *Then* he'd be fit enough to keep up with Ania.

"Did you say pastry?" Boris asked as they dodged a pair of the highest heels JR had ever seen. He hadn't realized he'd spoken aloud. "I'll bet you've never tasted *blini*, have you? It's a Russian staple—a paper-thin pancake slathered in sour cream or honey." Boris licked his lips. "We'll make sure to find you some, or at least find someone willing to part with theirs. Now, when we get back up to the street, be sure to look to your left, where you'll see an excellent example of neo-classical architecture ..."

They scampered out of the underpass, emerging onto another busy street. By now it was nighttime, but the city seemed nowhere near ready to sleep. Accordion music pulsed in a nearby restaurant. People walked in pairs and small groups, chatting and laughing and dressed for a night out. JR consulted with his stomach, determining that it was almost eight o'clock. He knew this because at eight o'clock each night, George would brew himself a cup of Sleepytime tea, and he and JR would snack on cookies together. JR's stomach had come to expect it.

"You're very lucky to live in the Arbat district," Boris informed him, bringing his attention back to the scene before him. "Although this particular street has lost much of its former glory. At one time, you see, it was home to servants of the Tsar, who lived in wooden houses. But these were burnt to the ground in 1812, when ..."

JR listened with half an ear while trying to keep an eye on the dogs ahead. As grateful as he was for Boris's kindness, he couldn't help wishing he was up ahead with Ania, learning about Moscow from her. He had a feeling her tour would be entirely different.

Eventually, she did fall back to check on them. "How's the tour, Embassy?" she asked without looking down at JR. Her eyes were constantly on the move, scanning the crowd around her.

For some reason, he didn't mind quite so much when she called him "Embassy." "Great," he said. "Informative," he added, for Boris's sake.

"I bet." The corners of her mouth twitched. "Boris, we're going to head for Arbatskaya."

"Oh." Boris looked dejected. "I was hoping to show JR the Pushkin Literary Museum and the Gallery of European and American Art of the 19th and 20th Centuries."

JR made a noise that he hoped sounded polite and interested.

"But I suppose we can do that later," said Boris. "Arbatskaya is very close to Red Square."

"And more importantly, the best food in the city," Ania added.

"Really?" JR asked. That sounded much better.

"Really." Ania nodded, scanning the crowd again. "The Kroshka Kartoshka stand is the place to be this time of night."

"All right, but just a quick stop. We have a lot of ground to cover at Red Square," said Boris.

Ania made a noise that sounded neither polite nor interested.

"Wait a sec. Ania, you're taking Embassy to Kroshka Kartoshka?" Fyodor appeared on her other side. "Come *on*! We don't want the whole world knowing about it!"

"I hardly think he's going to tell the whole world about it." She turned to JR. "Are you?" It was more a statement than a question.

"Uh, no," he said, and Ania gave Fyodor a look that said, "See?" Fyodor glared at JR.

Five minutes later, they were standing in front of a giant green and yellow box, inside of which a man was slopping all kinds of toppings on baked potatoes, like the one Ania had stolen from the man with the sunglasses. Judging by the long lineup in front of it, she was right. Kroshka Kartoshka *was* the place to be.

"'Kroshka Kartoshka' is a term of endearment," Boris informed him. "It means something like 'my little potato crumb.'"

"Really?" JR couldn't imagine why someone would want to be called a potato crumb. He wondered if George knew about this. It could be useful information if he ever wanted to impress a Russian girl.

Then he inhaled deeply, and the smell that flooded his nose was like nothing he'd ever experienced. It was a mixture—no, a *potpourri*—of potato and onion, cheese and pickles, hot dogs and eggplant stew. And *bacon*. Lots of bacon. A whimper escaped him before he could stop it.

"Exactly." Beside him, Ania took a deep breath, too. "There's no other way to put it."

"Does it taste as good as it smells?" JR asked.

"You mean you've never tried it?" she asked, incredulous. "Are you serious? You've never had Kroshka Kartoshka?"

JR shrugged, embarrassed. Usually, he was the one with the experiences that other dogs envied.

"Where'd you say you're from?"

"Canada," he said, then quickly added, "but we've moved around a lot. I've lived in Helsinki, Kuala Lumpur, Paris, and Dublin."

"Huh," she said. "Well, that's nice, but you haven't lived until you've had Kroshka Kartoshka."

She wasn't the least bit impressed by his globe-trotting. And strangely enough, he was glad for it.

"Okay, you know the Bark-and-Grab, right?" she asked.

"The what?"

"You *don't* know the Bark-and-Grab?"

He shook his head.

She sighed. "Fyodor, show Embassy a Bark-and-Grab."

"On it." Fyodor leaped up. He bounced on the pavement a few times, then jogged off toward the crowd.

"The Bark-and-Grab is one of the first food acquisition skills a stray learns," Ania said. "It's one of the most efficient ways of getting a meal. Watch."

Fyodor paused to study the people leaving the food stand, carrying their potatoes in cardboard boxes. Then he headed for a man in jeans and a leather jacket.

"He's chosen his victim," Ania whispered.

The man stopped and opened his box, then pulled out a plastic fork and went in for a big bite. Fyodor lowered himself closer to the ground, creeping toward him from behind. Closer ... and closer ...

"What's he going to—" JR whispered.

"Shh," Ania said, as if they might disrupt his concentration.

Just as the man was about to take his first bite, Fyodor let out a mighty bark, startling him so badly that he fumbled the box. In a split second, Fyodor was on it, snatching the potato right out of the air. He and the potato were gone before the man realized what had happened.

"Go, go!" Ania yelled as Fyodor sprinted by with his prize. They all raced after him, stopping around the corner near another underpass.

"Nice work!" said Ania.

"Yes, very good, Fyodor." Boris eyed the potato he'd dropped on the pavement. It was smothered in cheese and sour cream and what appeared to be slices of hot dog. JR's mouth watered.

"Too easy." Fyodor tossed his head. "Let's dig in."

But Boris stepped forward and put a paw on the potato. "JR must have the first bite," he said firmly. "He's never tried it before."

Fyodor sighed impatiently. "Only an embassy dog would have never tried Kartoshka before," he grumbled. But he stepped out of the way.

"Go on, son." Boris nudged JR. "You haven't lived until you've tried it."

JR darted forward and grabbed a mouthful before they could change their minds.

It was even better than he'd imagined. Tender and tangy, gooey and meaty. Everything a dog could want, all in one bite.

"Wow," he said once he'd gulped it down. "Oh, *wow*." The Kartoshka cloud in his brain left him unable to think of anything else to say.

"Exactly," said Ania. "Okay, boys, dig in."

"Thanks," JR added politely to Fyodor, who shrugged and proceeded to inhale his share.

After they'd devoured the potato, Boris looked around. "Well now," he said, "let's continue on to Red Square." He turned to Ania for approval. "No tour would be complete without it."

She sniffed the air. "Yeah, okay. I need to find Sasha anyway. He'll have the latest update." And she frowned.

Before JR could ask what the update was about, he was hit by yet another striking smell. But this was no stuffed potato. This was … He concentrated hard, trying to pick up the smell amongst fumes of onions and gasoline. Yes, that was it. Leather and a hint of cinnamon.

He spun around, and sure enough, there was George, standing on the sidewalk not twenty feet away, chatting with a man about his age. Conrad, most likely. As he watched, the two shook hands, slapped each other on the back, then parted ways. George yawned and checked his wrist for the time, only to find it bare. He shook his head, then began walking for home.

"Oh no!" JR whispered.

"What? What is it?" asked Boris.

"It's my human. He's on his way home. I have to go."

"But you haven't even seen Red Square! The Kremlin alone takes an entire night to explore!" Boris protested.

"I know, but ..." JR watched George amble off, hands in his pockets. Part of him wanted nothing more than to stay out and continue the adventure. But if George got home and found him gone, he might never have another walkie, let alone a night out. "I've got to go."

"All right," Boris sighed. "Shall we continue the tour tomorrow?"

Fyodor groaned softly, and Ania gave him a tired look. "I'm going to find Sasha," she said. "Nice meeting you, Embassy." And she trotted off without waiting for him to answer. Fyodor followed.

JR's heart sank as he watched her go. "Is she ... always this ..."

"Intense?" Boris finished. "Most of the time. But right now she's got a lot on her mind." He shook his head. "Tomorrow night, then?"

JR turned to the older dog. "Yes. Tomorrow. For sure." He had no idea what George would be doing tomorrow night, but he'd make it work. He had to. "Thanks, Boris."

"You're welcome. We'll meet you at the corner store. The one with the sausages," said Boris. "Now, you'd better get going."

JR nodded, then turned and raced after George, keeping a safe distance behind him all the way home. He waited in the shadows while George let himself into the apartment lobby, then leaped back into the open window, suddenly thankful to be an average-sized Jack Russell.

He was in bed by the time George slid the key in the lock and opened the door.

6
Crime and Punishment

He awoke to a scream, followed by a loud thump. JR leaped out of bed and stood on the cold tile, knees bent and ready for action. Sunlight was trickling through the window, which was still open a crack, letting chilly morning air into the living room.

For a moment, the apartment was perfectly still. But just as he was beginning to think he'd dreamed up the scream, there was a terrible roar.

"J-Aaaarrrrrrrrrrrrrrrr!"

George burst out of the bedroom, dressed in his pyjamas with the sailboat print. "My ... my ..." he sputtered, stumbling toward JR. "You ... you ..." Then his shoulders sagged and he held out his hand, revealing the remains of the Dumont-Sauvage Seafaring Nomad AC III.

JR swallowed hard and looked away. Outside the window, two women in fur hoods were pulling grocery carts down the sidewalk. How easy it would be to slip out and join them. He'd head for the corner store, then—

Memories of the previous night's adventures suddenly bombarded his brain, and his stomach turned a flip. Had he actually toured the neighbourhood with a pack of stray dogs? Yes. And not only that, he'd eaten the best food in the city! And learned the Bark-and-Grab!

He pulled his attention back to George, who was stamping his feet and pulling his hair and yelling something about meteorites and zero gravity. JR tried to feel bad about the pile of parts in George's hand, but all he really felt was joy. It was the kind of joy he'd felt chasing seagulls at Moira's cottage, except ... Yes, it was better.

And what's more, the adventures were just beginning. He'd promised Boris he'd meet him again that night. Just mere hours away!

JR sighed happily into the folds of his flannel bed, which smelled like potatoes and bacon. He must have brought the smells home with him the night before.

He inhaled deeply. Ah, Moscow.

That morning, George broke a record for Shortest Walkies Ever. Their after-work outing was pitiful, too. But it didn't matter. All those hours in the boring apartment didn't matter either, with the promise of adventure later on.

On the way home from their second walkies, George picked up a pizza for dinner. Back in the apartment, he opened the box and, out of habit, headed straight for JR's dish. Then he stopped, looked down at his bare wrist, and turned away with a grunt. He ate his pizza on the couch while JR sat near the window pretending not to notice. Who needed pizza anyway, when there was something as delicious as Kroshka Kartoshka out there?

He pitied George for not knowing about Kroshka Kartoshka.

"I'm going out tonight, boy," George said over a mouthful of pepperoni and cheese. It sounded more like "Um goon aw tenet baw." "Probably late," he added, swallowing. "You shouldn't wait up."

So he was playing *that* game. JR rolled his eyes. It was meant to make him feel bad, and a few days before, it might have worked. But today, it was exactly what he wanted to hear. He couldn't have planned it better himself.

"I met someone last night," George continued, wiping tomato sauce off his chin and unknowingly smearing it on his ear. "At the art exhibit. Her name's Katerina, and she seems great. We're going to a show."

JR rolled his eyes again. Katerina might have been great, but could she nab a potato right out of the air? With her teeth? He thought not.

Fortunately, George didn't dally. He was dressed and smelling like leather with a hint of cinnamon within half an hour. After he'd left, JR forced himself to wait—just in case George had left his phone or his pocket comb at home and had to come back.

When five of the longest minutes of his life had passed, he slipped out the open window and onto the cool pavement below.

This second evening was no less delightful than the first. The clouds were soft and pink around the edges, and whiffs of new grass mingled with the usual gasoline and cigarette smoke. JR let his hind legs dance their off-leash dance as he trotted off to the corner store. This time, he didn't flinch when humans passed by, knowing they wouldn't pay him any attention. He still didn't quite understand it, but it was just fine by him.

A miniature schnauzer walked by, tethered to its human by a tight leash. She gave JR a look of longing, and he returned one of sympathy. Then he danced off, wondering what the embassy dogs he'd met at the park were doing. In all likelihood, they were asleep beside fireplaces that weren't really fireplaces, dreaming about the dull walkies they'd take the next day. What would they say if they knew he was out with a pack of dirty, smelly, possibly flea-bitten strays? Beatrix would probably faint.

He considered telling them all about it at the park the next day, but quickly decided against it. The strays would be his little secret. And anyway, the embassy dogs would never understand.

But when he arrived at the corner store, there were no strays in sight. He checked a nearby alley and found it empty. He sniffed the air for a whiff of Boris, Ania, or Fyodor. No sign of any of them.

He sat and waited.

The sun dropped behind the buildings and the sky darkened. In the windows across the street, families were sitting down to dinner, telling each other about their day at school and work. JR's mouth watered and his paws twitched. What if the strays didn't come at all? What if Boris had lied? Or what if something had happened to them?

But just as he was starting to get very twitchy, the breeze shifted directions and he got a whiff of the sour stray smell that only two days before would have made his toes curl. Now, however, it made his tail spring skyward.

"My apologies," Boris said, drawing up beside him and pausing to catch his breath.

"That's okay!" JR leaped to his feet, greeting his new friend with a forgiving nose-butt. He looked around. "Where are the others?"

Boris frowned. "We'll catch up with them later, in Red Square. Ania had some business to attend to."

"Oh." JR wondered if it had anything to do with the update she'd mentioned the previous night. But he didn't want to pry. And what mattered most was that he'd see her later on. "To the Red Square, then?"

Boris grinned. "Prepare to be amazed."

When JR had pictured Red Square, he'd imagined a big red box, not unlike the green and yellow one that sold stuffed potatoes. But Red Square wasn't that kind of square at all. It was an enormous open area covered in uneven paving stones and rimmed with ornate buildings. Tourists wandered around, snapping photos of themselves in front of the buildings, and a few policemen stood by, keeping a close watch on everything. They didn't pay any more attention to the dogs than the other humans did.

"Welcome to Red Square!" Boris proclaimed. "This is the most important stop on any tour of the city!" The frown he'd worn upon meeting JR at the corner store had disappeared, and his eyes sparkled like a puppy's. Boris was obviously born to be a tour guide.

"Why is it called Red Square?" JR asked. "It doesn't look red."

"Excellent question!" said Boris. "You see, in Russian, the word 'red' isn't just a colour. It also means beautiful. And isn't this the most beautiful square you've ever seen?"

JR politely agreed, although it wasn't exactly his idea of beautiful. He considered telling Boris about the lush green grass and duck ponds in St. Stephen's Green, but decided against it. Instead, he tried to appreciate the stately brick and stone buildings around him.

"Let's start with St. Basil's Cathedral, the pièce de résistance of Red Square!" Boris led JR over to a massive church, whose colourful domes were all lit up against the night sky. It looked like one of the gingerbread houses George's Parisian girl-friend Sophie used to decorate in her bakery at Christmastime. JR had devoured one of those houses when Sophie and George were at midnight mass. He still maintained that it had served them right, leaving him alone on Christmas.

"St. Basil's was built for Ivan the Terrible, back in the 1500s," said Boris. "As you probably guessed, Ivan wasn't the kindest ruler. Legend has it that when St. Basil's was finished, he asked the architects who designed it if they could build another church just as beautiful. They told him yes, probably. And so he blinded them. So they could never build anything to rival this one."

JR's ears sprang up. "Really?"

Boris shrugged. "Legend has it. Now over here on your left, you'll see the Kremlin. Most cities in Russia have a kremlin, or had one at one time. 'Kremlin' simply means fortress. But this is *the* Kremlin, the most important—"

"Boris!"

JR turned to see Ania trotting toward them, sniffing the wind. His ears pricked up again. Behind her was Fyodor, his mouth crusted with sour cream. And behind him was a handsome black and white husky-type dog with serious brown eyes. Somehow, JR knew that this was Ania's friend Sasha. His ears lay back down.

"Ania!" Boris exclaimed, touching his nose to hers. "I'm glad you're here. JR and I were just getting into the wonders of the Kremlin, and I thought we'd—"

"Not now," Ania interrupted. "We've got to go."

"Go?" Boris repeated. "Go where?"

Ania's eyes flicked down to JR, then back up to Boris. "You know where," she said. "It's an emergency."

"Oh." Boris looked at the husky dog, who nodded gravely and stepped forward. He wasn't quite as tall as Ania, but he was muscular under all his fur. JR squared his shoulders and drew himself up to his fullest height, determined not to be intimidated.

"Hello." The dog gave JR a quick sniff. "I'm Sasha. I apologize for cutting into your tour."

JR's shoulders sank. Sasha was kind and polite as well as handsome. It was going to be hard to dislike him.

"That's okay," he sighed. "I'm JR."

"Nice to meet you. Ania tells me you're an embassy dog. Are you enjoying our city?"

JR nodded. "But I haven't seen much of it yet. We just got to Red Square."

"The tour will have to wait till another night, JR," said Boris. "I'm terribly sorry. But Headquarters is impressive, too. You'll see the—"

"What?" Fyodor cut in. "Embassy's coming to Headquarters? Are you crazy?"

"Headquarters?" JR said, looking from one stray to the next. Now he was thoroughly confused.

"Well, we can't very well leave him," Boris pointed out.

"Yes, but ..." Sasha gave JR a once-over, and JR drew himself up again.

"He's not one of us!" Fyodor growled.

But Ania silenced him with a curl of her lip. She turned to JR and regarded him for a minute. Finally, she said, "Can you keep a secret?" Again, it was more of a statement than a question. JR nodded. "Because you won't be allowed to tell anyone about where we take you."

JR gulped and nodded again, suddenly not so sure he wanted to be on this tour at all.

"All right, then." Ania turned to the others. "To Mayakovskaya."

7

The Only Way to Travel

Once again, they were off, dodging cars, weaving around feet, and ducking to avoid being smacked by briefcases and purses. JR tried his best to keep Ania's golden ears and Sasha's furry tail in his sights and ignore the voice in his head suggesting he might be better off back home in bed.

They headed down another ramp, into another dim maze of hallways. But this time, rather than running up another ramp back into the night, Ania led them down a wide staircase.

"Turn right up ahead," Boris called, bounding along behind JR. "We're headed for Ploshchad Revolutsii."

"But I thought Ania said we're going to May … Maya—"

"Mayakovskaya," said Boris. "She did. But we need to go to Revolutsii first."

"Oh" was all JR could say, for this meant next to nothing to him. He paused for a moment to look around, but a human leg pushed him on, hard.

"Keep going," Boris urged. "The humans won't wait for you. They're even pushier than usual in the metro."

JR ground to a full halt. "Wait, what? The *metro*?"

A canvas sneaker booted him in the rear end, and he jumped forward.

"Of course." Boris galloped past him. "It's the only way to travel. Hurry up now!" And he jumped down another set of stairs.

"You're kidding, right?" JR called, scampering after his tour guide. "We're not actually going to take the metro, are we?" He'd heard about the metro from George, who'd taken it to work in Paris. As he understood it, a metro system involved big, crowded trains rumbling through underground tunnels. And that was all he needed to know to be certain it wasn't the place for him.

"Of course!" Boris leaped down the last few steps and rounded a corner.

"But … but isn't the metro for … people?" JR gasped. He skidded around the corner and then stopped, finding himself in a large room lined with metal gates. People were queuing in front of the gates, each taking a turn holding a small card up to a big yellow button. Somehow, this made the doors within the gates fly open so that the people could pass through. Ania, Fyodor, and Sasha trotted right up to one of the queues.

"Wait," JR panted, trying to wrap his head around what they were about to do. "Don't we need tickets? I'm pretty sure my human buys tickets for the metro."

Boris chuckled and shook his head. "Watch." He pointed with his snout at Fyodor, who was sneaking up behind a human. Fyodor waited until she presented her card, and when the doors opened, he pressed through after her.

"Right. No tickets then," JR whispered, his heart pounding.

Following Boris's advice, he chose an older man wearing a big fur hat and slipped behind him, as close to the man's trousers as he dared. When the doors opened, he snuck through behind the man, bracing for the screams of offended humans.

But no one said a thing, or even seemed to notice. He shook his head in wonder, hurrying after the others. They rounded another corner and trotted across another room, toward a staircase leading even farther down.

Except this was not a normal staircase. This was a *moving* staircase. People were piling onto it, then standing still as it whisked them down, down,

down into the belly of the metro. JR craned his neck to see where it ended, but the staircase was so long and so steep that he couldn't tell. Beside it, another moving staircase was coming up, also packed with people.

"Escalators," he remembered George calling them. Again, not a way he cared to travel. But Ania, Sasha, and Fyodor had already hopped on, and Boris was nudging him from behind again. He had no choice but to swallow hard and follow.

He put a paw onto one of the steps, then drew it back. The step was vibrating. "I don't know about this," he whispered.

"No stopping." Boris head-butted him onto the next step, then hopped on behind him. "When I said the humans get pushy down here, I meant it. Don't worry, son. Just relax and enjoy the ride."

JR drew several deep breaths, trying to ignore the vibrations and the metal ridges underfoot that dug into his paws. The strays probably had such calloused paws that they didn't even feel them. JR cringed, suddenly reminded of George's soft, well-moisturized hands. Hopefully George was in no hurry to return home tonight. Who knew how long the meeting at Headquarters would take?

"The Moscow metro system is 308 kilometres long, with 186 stations," Boris told him as the escalator finally approached its end. "Humans began building it in the 1930s, with the aim of creating an underground work of art. Come, you'll see." The escalator met flat ground, and JR was only too happy to disembark.

"Whoa." He had to stop again. *"This* is a metro station?"

When George had talked about the metro in Paris, JR had imagined dark, narrow corridors and dirty waiting platforms. But Ploshchad Revolutsii was nothing like that. Its domed ceilings and red marble arches were lit by soft white lights, and its grey and black checkered floor gleamed underfoot. Along each side of the hallway stood life-sized brass statues of all kinds of humans, from farmers to athletes to children. JR stopped next to a statue of a soldier and his dog, then watched as a young man in jeans paused as well. The young man reached up and rubbed the dog's nose, then continued on his way. Obviously, it was some kind of a ritual, judging by how shiny the dog's nose was.

"They do that for good luck," Boris told him.

JR shook his head, taking it all in. "It's kind of like a palace down here."

"Exactly!" Boris looked pleased. "The metro stations were built as 'palaces for the people,' meant to show the commoners what could be achieved if they all worked together to drive the economy." He shrugged. "That didn't entirely work, but at least we got some nice stations out of it. Now come. I hear the train."

They caught up with Ania, Sasha, and Fyodor on the waiting platform just as a blue and grey train thundered up to it and screeched to a halt. The doors slammed open and people began to spill out.

"Hurry now," Boris said. "The doors won't wait, and you don't want to be caught between them when they shut." The four of them all hopped on board.

JR hesitated. Every part of him, from his toe-nails to his ear tufts, was telling him that dogs were not meant to ride big, rumbly underground trains. His legs began to shake and his mouth went dry, just as it had in—

The Hold. That was it. Getting on this train would be just like travelling in the belly of a thun-dering plane. He took a step back, then another, remembering the darkness, the unexpected bumps, the roar of the engines.

"JR, come quickly," Boris called from inside the door.

But he couldn't. His paws felt glued to the marble floor.

"It's safe!" Sasha added. "Come on!"

JR wasn't sure he actually *could* move, even if he wanted to. But what would he do if he stayed?

He couldn't very well go home. He had no idea where home even was.

"JR, come on!" Ania yelled, peering out the door.

"The doors are about to close!" cried Boris.

JR swallowed hard, closed his eyes, and made a break for it. He leaped into the waiting train just half a second before the doors slammed shut, nearly taking off his tail.

The train lurched forward, and he flattened himself on the floor. Ania watched him for a moment, then shook her head and walked off.

"It's all right, son," Boris told him quietly. "No dog is comfortable riding the train at first. But you'll get used to it." He followed Ania down the aisle between rows of seats, and JR had no choice but to force himself to stand and do the same. The floor was coated in dirt and littered with wrappers and crumpled newspapers, and it kept shifting under his paws—presumably as they rounded corners on the track. And the noise was awful: a constant rumbling, like a thunderstorm that wouldn't let up.

Ania and Sasha chose a spot on the floor next to an empty Kroshka Kartoshka box, but Fyodor actually hopped up onto the seats. He sprawled out and almost instantly began to snore. Some people on the seats opposite him paused for a moment to regard him with disdain, then went back to their conversation.

JR chose a spot on the floor across the aisle from Ania and Sasha. He tried to concentrate on not getting sick to his stomach.

"The metro is the only way to travel," Boris said again, scratching his ear with his hind leg. "It lets us access the entire city. Especially the places with the best food."

"You see, JR," said Sasha, "we don't think humans should be the only ones to benefit from the metro. It should be for everyone. And we think that whoever built the palaces for the common-ers would agree." He looked at Ania, who nodded. A man passing by dropped half an egg sandwich on the floor in front of her. She considered it a moment, then wolfed it down.

JR couldn't argue with that.

His legs had just barely stopped shaking when a woman's voice suddenly reverberated all around them. He looked up and around but couldn't tell who'd spoken.

"What was that?" he asked.

"The next-stop announcer," said Boris. "Here's a trick. Even if you don't understand what they're saying, you can always tell which way you're headed by listening to that voice. If it's a man's voice, you're going into the centre of the city. If it's a woman, you're headed out."

"That's because most people live in the suburbs and work in the centre," said Sasha. "The
man's voice is supposed to be like your boss calling you to work, and the woman's voice is like your
wife calling you home."

"An excellent illustration of archaic gender
stereotyping," Ania said, assuming the formal voice
of a tour guide. "Humans," she added with disgust.

JR paused and listened for the next announce-
ment. "Okay, so we're headed away from the centre.
But where exactly are we going?"

"To the Headquarters of the Metro Dogs of
Moscow," Sasha said, as if that explained it all. "It's
at Mayakovskaya, the most beautiful station in all
of Moscow."

"Really? You mean the one we were just at
wasn't the nicest?"

"Hardly." Sasha glanced at Ania. "Now, will
you excuse us, JR? Ania and I have a lot to discuss
before the meeting."

He and Ania stood and moved away, heads
bent together, leaving JR with a dozen more questions and a sour feeling in his gut. What did Sasha
have that he didn't, anyway? Other than height,
muscles, and good looks, of course.

Finally, the voice announced Mayakovskaya
station, and Fyodor rose and shook himself,

showering dirt on the woman beside him, who tried to whack him with her purse. Ania, Sasha, and Boris stationed themselves at the door.

The doors slammed open, and they were off again. JR tried not to stop as he took in the steel and pink stone columns and the pink patterns on the marble floors. He craned his head to see the mosaics high overhead, but there was no time to admire them, not with the metro dogs darting through the crowd ahead of him.

This time, though, they didn't take the escalator up onto the street. Instead, Sasha led them down a hall, at the end of which was a black door. He nosed it open and they filed inside, then down a staircase and along another corridor. Finally, when JR was certain he'd never, ever be able to find his way back out, they stopped in front of yet another door, this one heavy and wooden.

Sasha lifted a paw and scratched the door twice, paused, then scratched again.

"Who's there?" came a voice on the other side.

"Sasha," he replied. "I've got Ania and Boris and others."

"Password?" asked the voice inside.

"Bezdomnaya sobaka," Sasha answered.

"What does that mean?" JR whispered to Boris, recognizing the word "sobaka" as something the man with the sunglasses had said.

"It means 'stray dog,'" Boris whispered. "*Bezdomnaya* means stray, and *sobaka* means dog."

The door swung open, and Sasha led them inside.

8

The Metro Dogs of Moscow

At first glance, it was a grand and beautiful room. An enormous crystal chandelier hung from the centre of its very high ceiling. The walls were painted deep red and decorated with old paintings framed in gold, each one depicting some scene from the past—farmers labouring in a field, schoolchildren in a classroom, workers in a factory.

On closer inspection, however, it wasn't nearly as grand as it seemed. Not any more, anyway. For one thing, there was the smell—that sour stray smell JR was now almost used to. For another, there was the carpet, which at one time must have been plush and cream coloured, but was now threadbare and the colour of dirt.

And finally, there were the couches. Not only were they just as filthy and worn as the carpet, they were covered with stray dogs.

There were big dogs and small dogs, long-haired dogs and short-haired dogs, and even one hairless dog. There were retriever-type dogs and shepherd-ish dogs and hound-like dogs, all lounging on the furniture as if they owned the place.

"Palaces for the people," Boris had called the metro stations. This, however, was obviously a palace for the pooches. A castle for the canines. JR snickered at his own joke, then stopped when he realized that every dog in the room was staring directly at him.

"Ania." A stocky black hound with white freckles on his snout closed the door behind them. "We're glad you're here. Sasha and Boris, too." He gave Fyodor a wary look as he leaped up on the nearest couch, shouldering other dogs out of the way. Then he turned to JR. "Who is this?"

"JR," Ania said, walking into the middle of the room. "He's a new friend. We were showing him around the city." She flicked her long ears in an "I dare you to argue" kind of way, and several dogs nodded. One hopped off a couch to make room for her.

"Welcome, then," said the hound. "I am Sergei."

"Nice to meet you." JR tried to look serious, but all he wanted to do was let his hind legs dance. Ania had called him a friend!

"Well then, if everyone is here, I hereby call this meeting of the Metro Dogs of Moscow to order," Sergei announced. JR followed Boris to a spot on the carpet, where he had a good view of everyone. The metro dogs sat tall on their couches, ears pricked.

"You all know why you've been summoned. More dogs have disappeared in the past week, and we need to discuss what we know about the situation."

Disappearing dogs! JR stopped looking around and gave Sergei his full attention.

A few started to murmur among themselves, and Sergei held up a paw. "One at a time. Sasha, why don't you start."

Sasha cleared his throat. "No one's seen Vlad for two weeks now," he reported. "And Anastasia for three. Both were last seen around Tverskaya."

Sergei thought for a moment, then said, "That brings the count to twenty-five."

A dainty grey terrier with enormous black eyes stood up. JR could tell right away that she was an adorable-but-vicious type. He'd met a lot of those in Paris.

"I can't help but think we're worrying about nothing," she said, licking her paw. "Maybe they've just found someplace nice, and they're not telling the rest of us about it."

"I agree," said a slightly dim-looking retriever. "I heard that a dog food company went out of business and abandoned an entire warehouse of food, somewhere in the suburbs. Maybe all the missing dogs are there, feasting on kibble."

The hairless dog whimpered. "Could it be true?"

"I'll bet it's chicken and rice," moaned a skinny shepherd. "I *love* chicken and rice."

A long-haired blond dog stood up on her couch and tossed her hair.

"Oksana?" Sergei said.

"Impossible," Oksana proclaimed. "I know Anastasia better than anyone. If she found a warehouse full of kibble, every dog in Moscow would know about it in an hour. She can't keep a secret to save her life."

A few dogs chuckled and agreed.

"I heard," Oksana continued, "that city workers are shipping strays to control camps outside the city. They think there are too many of us."

"Is that like the pound?" the skinny shepherd asked.

"It's worse than the pound," Oksana answered. "There's next to no food at these camps and no clean water. And the cages are tiny—so small you can barely turn around inside them. If you end up there, you won't last two weeks."

The shepherd gulped.

The dogs began to murmur again. The hairless one whined. The dim-looking retriever insisted they stay positive. Ania kept quiet, but her grey eyes were grim. Even Fyodor looked uncertain.

"But I thought humans didn't mind strays here," JR blurted out, then shrank back as everyone turned to look at him. The words had escaped before he could think better of interrupting the meeting. "Sorry," he mumbled. "I just thought ..."

"It's not that simple, Embassy," Fyodor snapped.

"Fyodor." Boris shot him a warning look.

"It is complicated, JR." Sergei sat back on his haunches. "Moscow has always had many strays. At one time, decades ago, the government would kill them to keep them under control."

"Barbarians." Oksana shook her long, blond head, and the dim-looking retriever let out a quiet, mournful howl.

"Eventually, though," Sergei went on, "the Russian people decided they'd had enough of that government. And with the new one came new rules—or rather, no rules for strays. We were allowed to live where we wanted and go where we pleased. And we still do."

"Hear, hear." Sasha thumped his thick tail on the carpet.

"The problem," Sergei continued, "is that these days, there are more and more of us—some say too many. But it's not our fault. It's the fault of all those humans who think they need big, impressive dogs for their big, impressive lives. But they don't know how to raise them or care for them. And when they realize that having a dog is hard work, well ..." Sergei sighed.

"What?" JR asked, although he had a good idea.

"The dogs get thrown out onto the streets," Ania finished.

"Really?" JR shivered, imagining what would happen if George decided one day that he was too much trouble. Then he remembered the Dumont-Sauvage Seafaring Nomad AC III, and swore to himself that he'd never destroy anything again.

Somehow, Boris read his thoughts. "It's getting late, JR," he murmured. "Do you have to be getting home?"

JR consulted with his stomach. Eight o'clock had come and gone long ago, and he'd barely noticed. It was probably close to ten now. He glanced around, wanting to stay and learn more, but knowing he couldn't. "Yeah. I do."

"I'll take you, then," said Boris. "You'd never find it on your own, and frankly, I'm not sure how much more of this I can listen to." He sighed. "Come."

The others had gone back to speculating about possible reasons for the disappearances, so barely anyone noticed when Boris and JR excused themselves and headed back out the heavy door. Boris led the way down the corridor and up the stairs to the main station.

Back on the train, JR turned to the older dog, who was looking even older than usual. "Can I ask you a question?"

"Of course," said Boris, straightening a little.

"Sergei said that humans are always buying dogs for the wrong reasons, then kicking them out, right?"

Boris nodded sadly.

"So all those dogs back there once had their own humans?"

"Some," Boris replied. "Fyodor did. I did, too. In fact, I used to be a very handsome dog, if you'll believe it. A prime specimen." He held his head up and peered down at JR.

"Wow." JR tried hard to picture it.

"Wow, indeed. Only the heartiest dogs survive being abandoned. Many more perish."

JR thought for a moment, then asked, "Was Ania thrown out, too?"

Boris shook his head. "She was born on the street." Then he chuckled. "You don't want to mess with our Ania."

Boris left him at the corner store where they'd first seen each other. It felt like weeks ago.

"Can we try again tomorrow for the tour?" JR asked.

For a moment, Boris looked concerned. Then he nodded. "All right. You really must see the Kremlin. Same time, same place?"

"Same time, same place," said JR, and he turned for home.

9

Uninvited Company

"Where ya been, JR?" Robert the Australian shepherd asked at the park the next day. "Haven't seen you much lately."

"What's that?" JR shook himself out of his thoughts, which were riding a metro someplace far away. "Oh. Well. I …"

"He found out, didn't he?" Beatrix cut in, searching for a dry spot on the grass where she could sit without getting dirty.

"Who what?" JR cocked his head.

"Your human," said Beatrix. "He found out what you did."

"Oh. Oh!" JR looked up at George, who was telling Johanna Van Wingerden and John Cowley about the art exhibit he'd seen a couple nights back. "Actually, yeah. He's been cutting the walkies—I mean, walks—pretty short."

Beatrix sniffed in a serves-you-right kind of way, but Pie gave JR a sympathetic look.

"He'll come around," he assured him. "John always does. Even the time I ate the collar off his best suit."

Robert chuckled at the memory. "So I guess you haven't been out exploring much?"

"Of course not," JR said quickly. "Why?"

Robert shrugged. "No reason. John took us on a new walk yesterday. Down some different streets, to what I think he said was the theatre district. Kinda interesting."

"It was an adventure," Pie said, wide-eyed. "The ballet had just let out, and there were all these humans dressed to the nines."

"The ballet is a *very* big deal in Moscow," Beatrix said knowingly.

JR pitied the shepherds for thinking that an on-leash walk to the theatre district counted as exploring the city. Part of him was dying to tell them about his own adventures—*real* adventures. But that would be too dangerous. What if they wanted to come along?

Fortunately, George soon tugged on his leash, ready to go home. Apparently, his date with Katerina had gone so well the previous night that he'd set up another that very evening. And he hadn't even made a move to close the open window near JR's bed.

It was almost too easy.

"See ya, boy. Don't wait up," George said as he headed to the door, smelling like a hefty dose of leather and cinnamon. He paused near the closet and reached up for the box of treats, then glanced down at his bare wrist. Shaking his head, he left the treats where they were and walked out the door, locking it behind him.

JR's mouth watered for only a minute or two, while he waited until the coast was clear. Then he tossed his head and launched himself out the window. He'd find his own treats, thank you very much.

He headed for the corner store, as usual. Tonight, though, the sky was grey and the air smelled like approaching rain showers. He picked up the pace, wondering if he'd actually get to see the Kremlin that night, or if there might be another emergency meeting to attend. Could more dogs have disappeared overnight?

"JR! *JR!*"

He froze in his tracks, then turned slowly in the direction of the voice, which was coming from a nearby apartment building. What he saw made his stomach drop. Robert the Australian shepherd was nudging open one of the first-floor windows. "J!" He poked his head out the window. "It *is* you!"

"Oh no!" JR whispered. Assuming an innocent look, as if his being off-leash on the sidewalk was no big deal, he stepped toward the window. "Hey, Robert."

"What the heck are you doing out there?" Robert asked, now half-hanging out the window. "And without a leash? Where's George?"

JR shushed him. "Not so loud. I'm just—"

"Robert, who's that?" Pie's head appeared at the window too. "JR!" he cried. "It's JR! Robert, what's he doing out there?"

"Not sure," said Robert. "What are ya doing, J?"

JR sighed, kicking himself for not taking a back alley. "I'm ... I'm just ... going out. Exploring a bit."

"Exploring!" Robert's ears pricked up. "Off-leash?"

Pie's eyes widened. "By yourself?"

"Well, yeah," said JR. "But not very far," he added. "Maybe just to the corner and back. Nowhere very interesting." The last thing he wanted was sheltered embassy dogs tagging along on his adventure.

"You just slipped through the window?" Robert asked, inspecting the one he was half-leaning out of.

JR nodded, glancing behind him. "But look, I should get going—"

"Hang on. We're coming." Robert began to heave himself over the windowsill.

"What?" JR's mouth dropped open. This was definitely not part of the plan.

"We are?" Pie squeaked. "Oh no, Robert. What if we get lost?"

But Robert was already on the pavement. His eyes gleamed. "We won't get lost. But you don't have to come, Pie. We won't be long."

"But … but how will we get back in?" Pie wailed.

"Shh. I'll give you a boost. And I can leap like nobody's business," said Robert. "Our dad was the top agility dog in all of Australia," he added to JR.

"Wait, what about your human?" JR asked, thinking fast. "What about John? He'll be furious."

"He's out," said Robert. "After dinner, he always goes back to work and stays there till late. He won't miss us. Pie, you coming?"

"Oh!" Pie moaned, his breath fogging up the window. "Oh, I don't know. You know I hate being alone. But …" He looked down at the ground, then back at the living room behind him. "Okay. But not for long, right?" He tumbled out the window, landing on his rear end on the pavement. "Ow."

"Right then." Robert winked at JR. "Let's go exploring!"

JR's heart sank. "Wait ..." he began, but he couldn't think of any way to convince them not to come. "All right," he sighed, and led them down the street, consoling himself that at least it was only the shepherds tagging along, and not the prim and proper Beatrix.

No sooner had the thought crossed his mind than a tapping noise made them all turn.

"No *way!*" JR moaned. For there was Beatrix, standing in a window, lips pursed and eyes narrowed.

She shoved the window open and squeezed her fuzzy head through the gap. "*What* do you think you're doing?" she demanded. "Where are your humans and your leashes? Where are you going?"

Pie cowered behind Robert, who grinned. "We're going adventuring!" he announced.

JR sighed again. But there was no way Beatrix would come. She'd never disobey Johanna Van What's-her-name.

"Not without me, you're not!" Beatrix declared, pushing the window open some more. The next thing they knew, a large ball of fluff was rolling out the window onto the pavement.

Beatrix picked herself up and smoothed her whiskers. "Now. Where are we going?"

JR couldn't believe it. "But ... but w-what about Johanna?" he sputtered. "You wouldn't leave her, would you?"

"Already in bed," Beatrix replied, checking her nails for scratches. "The woman sleeps like the dead."

JR's heart plummeted. What was he going to do? He couldn't take them on the metro—Pie would have a heart attack. And he definitely wasn't going to introduce them to Boris and Ania and the others. That would be a disaster.

"It's going to be dirty," he warned Beatrix. "*Very* dirty."

She hesitated, then pointed her nose skyward. "I'm *very* good at staying clean."

JR choked back a whine. He'd just have to take them someplace close by, then bring them straight home. And then, he'd head back out himself—taking the back alley this time.

"So, where we going, J?" Robert asked, stretching his hind legs one at a time.

"Um …" JR thought fast. "To the Pushkin Literary Museum."

"The what?" Pie whispered, as if JR had just announced he was taking them to the pound.

"A literary museum?" Robert stopped stretching. "Why?"

"Because it's a cultural experience," Beatrix informed him.

"Oh." Pie chewed on his lip. "Will it be frightening?"

"Frighteningly boring, probably," Robert told him.

"I think it'll do you both some good," said Beatrix. "Come on, JR. Show us the way."

They set off down the street, JR congratulating himself on his quick thinking. Even though he didn't actually know where the Pushkin *was*, he could choose any old building and pretend they'd reached their destination. He'd bore them to tears with made-up facts on Russian literature, then bring them right back home. And if he played his cards just right, they'd never want to come out again.

10
A Cultural Experience

With JR leading the way, they headed in the same direction he'd taken the night before. Robert zipped back and forth across the sidewalk, sniffing everything in his path, and Pie stuck close to his side, eyes darting around as if he expected one of the humans to nab him any minute.

"You've obviously been out by yourself before," Beatrix observed, looking down at JR. "Why didn't you tell us?"

"Yeah, J." Robert stopped to smell a cigarette butt. "There you were, pretending that you never get to go off-leash. You sly dog." He wrinkled his nose at the cigarette, then moved on to inspect a candy wrapper just off the sidewalk. A car careened around a corner, nearly swiping off his snout, and he jumped back with a whoop.

"I've only been out a few times," JR told them. "And it wasn't very interesting," he added, remembering the metro rides and the top-secret meeting. He couldn't wait to take the embassy dogs home, then find his new friends and help them crack the case of the missing strays. "Come on, let's hurry."

The sidewalks grew busier the farther they walked. Soon, they were surrounded by marching feet, whizzing cars, and all kinds of smells, from the pastries in people's shopping bags to the mothballs that preserved their fur coats.

"I can't believe we've never done this before!" Robert crowed, taking a whiff of a passing sneaker. "This is amazing! Off-leash is the way to go!"

"Oh, I don't know," Pie panted, stumbling after his brother. "Don't you miss the leash, even just a tiny bit?"

"Well, it certainly is … cultural," Beatrix commented, eyeing a pair of blue leather pumps. "Look at all those fancy clothes. But why don't these humans care that we're out here on our own? It's like they don't even see us." She tossed her big hair, as if trying to get noticed.

JR shrugged. "Like our humans said: there's a lot of strays in Moscow."

Beatrix looked appalled. "But surely they don't think … they can't think we're *strays*!" She stopped as another thought came to mind. "Do you think we'll actually *meet* any?" She shuddered.

"I hope not," JR said, and he meant it—particularly if the strays were Ania, Boris, and Fyodor. Beatrix might faint at the sight of their dirty coats. Robert would probably ask embarrassing questions. And Pie, well, they'd have to peel him off the ground.

"This is awesome, JR!" Robert yelled, pouncing on a half-eaten orange. "Ha *ha!* Isn't it awesome, Pie? Aren't you glad you didn't stay home?"

"Thrilled!" Pie squeaked, leaping sideways to avoid a leaf skittering across the sidewalk. "And speaking of home, when do you think we'll be turning back?"

"We're just getting started!" Robert answered, taking off after an unsuspecting pigeon.

"I was afraid of that," sighed Pie. "Robert, wait!"

They passed the restaurant that smelled like pork stew and the spot where the skinny man had grabbed JR two nights before. Most of the humans were headed in the same direction, so he let himself be swept along. Soon, they were strolling along the street where the Tsar's servants once lived in their wooden houses, according to Boris. JR looked around for a building that would pass for a literary museum.

"Whoa! What is *that?*" Robert ground to a halt, drawing in big gulps of air. "J, do you smell that?"

Indeed he did. The familiar cloud of potato and sour cream and bacon descended on his brain, making him drool. They had to be nearing a Kroshka Kartoshka stand.

Pie whimpered. Beatrix gasped. "What *is* that?" she asked. "I've never smelled anything like it."

"It's called Kroshka Kartoshka," JR told them. "It's basically a big stuffed potato. Now come on, I think the Pushkin's just up—"

"Are you kidding?" said Robert. "Who cares about the Pushkin when there's krosh-whatever-you-called-it around. I want some of *that*!"

Beatrix licked her lips. "Maybe ... maybe Robert's right. The Pushkin can wait, can't it? After all, this is a cultural experience in itself."

Pie whimpered again and nodded.

JR sighed. As much as he wanted to reach their destination and then zip right back home, he certainly couldn't blame them for wanting Kroshka Kartoshka. It was, after all, the most delicious thing on earth.

Plus, he now knew the Bark-and-Grab. And wouldn't the embassy dogs be impressed to see him steal a stuffed potato!

"All right," he told them. "This way."

Once again, the big green and yellow box was surrounded by hungry humans. The lineup was even longer than last time.

"Okay." JR took a deep breath, trying to remember exactly how Fyodor had done it. "You guys wait here. I'll see what I can do." And he trotted off toward the storefront, assessing the humans streaming out of it.

He chose a short, bald man in running shoes and sweatpants, who was talking on his phone while opening his box. JR slipped behind him and followed for a few paces, gathering his courage.

His chance came when the man paused at the curb to cross the street. JR took a deep breath, bent his knees so he'd be ready to pounce on the falling potato, and let out the biggest, mightiest bark he could muster.

The man didn't even notice. Taking a big bite, he stepped into the intersection and walked away.

JR's tail sagged. How embarrassing! He looked around, hoping no one else had witnessed the World's Worst Bark-and-Grab. At least the embassy dogs wouldn't have known what he was trying to do. He could tell them it was all part of the plan.

That's when he heard laughter. All-too-familiar laughter.

"Bark-and-Grab *fail*!" someone hollered.

"Oh no," he whispered, whirling around.

About ten feet away, Fyodor was rolling on his back, laughing. Beside him, Boris was trying to look sympathetic, but the corners of his mouth were twitching. Even Ania's grey eyes looked amused.

"Ha *ha!*" Fyodor yelled, trotting over. "That might've been the funniest thing I've ever seen. Was that seriously your best bark? It couldn't have been! Ha ha!"

JR shrugged and looked down at a crack in the pavement, wishing it might open up and swallow him.

"A word of advice, Embassy," Fyodor said. "Leave the Bark-and-Grabs to the big dogs. You're better suited to the Sit-and-Look-Cute."

"The what?" JR mumbled miserably.

"The Sit-and-Look-Cute." Fyodor grinned. "It's when you just sit there and bat your eyelashes until someone gives you food. Best suited for small dogs," he added, and JR's ears burned.

"Now, now," said Boris, coming to stand beside JR. "The Sit-and-Look-Cute is a perfectly honourable acquisition strategy. It's an excellent way to get food without exerting yourself."

Fyodor snorted.

"Ahem." Behind JR, someone cleared his throat. He turned and jumped at the sight of Robert, Pie, and Beatrix. In all his embarrassment, he'd forgotten about them.

"Oh. Um ..." JR looked from the strays to the embassy dogs, lost for words. What on earth had he been thinking, taking them on a tour?

"Hey, wait a second." Fyodor looked around. "Are these more embassy dogs?" He turned to Ania. "I knew it! He *did* go and tell the world about Kroshka Kartoshka!" He turned back to JR. "That's how you repay us? We took you to *Headquarters*!"

"What? No! I—" JR began.

"JR," Robert whispered. "You know these guys?"

"Well, yeah, I—" JR began again.

"What's Headquarters?" asked Beatrix.

"Nothing. I just—"

"Or maybe he's just bringing the purebreds out to look at all the strays," Fyodor sneered. "Is that what you're up to?"

"Strays?" Pie gasped. He looked at Beatrix. "They're strays? Didn't you say that strays have rab—"

"No!" JR yelled. His head was starting to throb, and he couldn't bring himself to look up at Ania. "We're just out for a walk, that's all."

"Yeah, right!" Fyodor took a menacing step forward, and Pie darted behind his brother, tail between his legs.

"That's enough!" Boris cut in. "Fyodor, mind your manners. There's more than enough food to go around. And I'm sure JR didn't bring his friends out to see the strays. Did you, JR?"

"Of course not!"

"Actually, he was just taking us to some literary museum," Robert put in. "But hey, if you can suggest someplace more—"

Boris's eyes lit up. "The Pushkin! Yes, of course, we missed it on our tour yesterday. JR, I didn't realize you were so interested. But you're headed in the wrong direction! No matter, we'll take you. Won't we?" He turned to Fyodor, who groaned.

"Ania?" Boris looked over at her.

But Ania wasn't even paying attention. "Sure, whatever," she replied, staring at something in the distance.

"Excellent. Now JR, please introduce your friends."

"Oh," JR sighed. "This is Beatrix. She's from the Netherlands."

Beatrix nodded, eyeing Boris's scar. She shot JR a look that said, "Are you sure about this?"

"And this is Robert and Pie. They're from Australia."

"Nice to meet ya," said Robert, sniffing each stray in turn. Pie, predictably, flattened himself like a pancake on the pavement. Robert rolled his eyes and turned to JR. "So, what's Headquarters?"

"Um …" JR looked at Fyodor, who glared at him.

"It's where we have our meetings," Boris answered, glancing at Ania to make sure she approved.

"What kind of meetings?" asked Robert.

"All kinds," said Boris. "Lately, we've been discussing how strays are disappearing across the city."

"Disappearing?" Beatrix repeated. "How? Why?"

"That's enough," Ania suddenly snapped. "I don't want to talk about it."

A heavy silence fell over them, as awkward as the wool coat George used to make JR wear in Helsinki. He cringed, both at the silence and the memory of the coat.

Fortunately, Robert quickly cleared the air. "Hey, any chance we can get some of that krosh-stuff for the road?" he asked.

"Yes, of course." Boris looked relieved. "Fyodor, a Bark-and-Grab?"

Fyodor looked at Ania, who shrugged and nodded. He sighed and trotted off.

Five minutes later, they were feasting in a nearby alley.

"Oh, *man*!" Robert exclaimed over a mouthful. "I knew it'd be good, but I didn't know it'd be this good! Thanks, Fy!"

Fyodor grunted but didn't look up from his meal. Pie, who'd finally peeled himself off the ground, was trying to suppress his whimpers as he tore into his share. Even Beatrix was eating with gusto, and didn't even notice that she was standing in a mud puddle.

But JR could only pick at his share, still kicking himself for ever agreeing to show the embassy dogs around. Adventures were definitely best had on his own.

"The Pushkin Literary Museum honours Alexander Pushkin, often considered the greatest Russian poet who ever lived," Boris explained as they walked on, bellies full of stuffed potato. "Pushkin was born in 1799 and died in 1837, but within that short time, he changed the face of modern literature."

Beatrix listened intently while keeping a safe distance, obviously concerned about fleas. Robert, meanwhile, was lagging behind, more interested in Fyodor's attempts to steal food out of passing grocery carts than in the man who changed the face of Russian literature. Fyodor seemed to appreciate the attention, even allowing Robert to try it himself. Pie still stuck close to his brother's side and didn't make a peep.

JR watched them over his shoulder and couldn't help feeling a bit sour in his belly, just as he had the previous night watching Sasha and Ania. Robert had only known Fyodor for half an hour, and already he was better friends with the stray than JR was. His ears still burned at the memory of his failed Bark-and-Grab.

"What's this?" Beatrix asked Boris, nodding at a crowd of people up ahead. They seemed to be inspecting the wall of a bus shelter.

"Easy pickings, that's what," Fyodor said. "C'mon, Robert. Let's go get dessert." He slipped into the crowd, and Robert trotted after him with Pie close behind.

"Looks like art," Ania said, stopping beside JR. At three times his height, she had a much better view. "There are some big pictures on the bus shelter."

"Ah!" said Boris. "Filip Filipov strikes again. Come, let's go see." He pushed his way into the crowd.

"Filip Filipov?" Beatrix repeated. "Is he very famous?"

"In some circles," Boris replied. "He's a very mysterious man. He never has traditional exhibits in galleries. Instead, he displays his art wherever he pleases. He rarely appears in public, and when he does, he's always disguised somehow. Very few people actually know what he looks like."

"Filip Filipov," JR repeated. This must have been the "Phil" whose art George had seen the night before. He squeezed himself between a pair of tall boots and emerged at the front of the crowd.

Filip Filipov's art was ... interesting. He seemed to take photographs and alter them on the computer—like George did, but to greater effect. The result was a colourful mess of landscapes and people that didn't look quite real.

"Filipov's work always makes some statement on Moscow, or Russia, or humans in general," Boris remarked. "JR, do you remember the art you saw last night?"

"Sure," said JR, thinking of the paintings on the walls at Headquarters.

"Remember how they showed people working together, on farms and in factories? Filipov, you see, is doing the same thing."

JR squinted at one of the pictures. It was indeed a farm landscape, but inside it were people who didn't belong at all. One man wore a suit, a few more people were dressed in swimming trunks, and one even appeared to be dancing in a tutu. In the bottom right-hand corner were two bright blue *F*'s, placed back to back. Filipov's signature, JR gathered.

"I see," he said. "But I don't really get it."

"Oh, I do," Beatrix said quickly. "It's very cultural."

JR rolled his eyes.

"Boris, I have to get out of this crowd." Ania sounded agitated. Once again, her eyes were on the move, scanning the crowd. "Let's get the others and go."

"All right," said Boris. To Beatrix he admitted, "This isn't really my kind of art anyway. Too modern for me. I much prefer the classics."

"Oh yes, me too," Beatrix agreed, hurrying after him.

Once the brothers and Fyodor had been rounded up, they continued on to the Pushkin, and JR took the opportunity to sidle up to Ania.

"Um ... are you okay?" he asked tentatively.

"What? Oh." She looked down as if seeing him for the first time. "Actually, no. Remember last night's meeting?"

He nodded. How could he forget?

"Well, just since then, two more dogs have disappeared. And one of them," she lowered her voice, "was Sergei."

JR gasped, remembering the black hound with the freckled snout.

Ania nodded, looking grim. "I just don't know what to do about it. But I know this can't go on. I've *got* to get to the bottom of it."

JR opened his mouth to volunteer to help, then paused. What could he—an average-sized

Jack Russell who didn't know the city—do to help? Still, he wanted to do *something*.

Thunder rumbled in the clouds overhead, and he shuddered. He hated thunder. Beatrix obviously felt the same, for she paused and looked back at him with wide eyes.

A few big drops splattered on the ground in front of him. Another caught him right between the eyes. Fyodor and the brothers came running over just as it began to pour. Pie was shivering, still glued to Robert's side.

"Looks like a storm," said Ania. "You'd all better get home."

Boris sighed. "Once again, our Pushkin plans are foiled. But yes, you should run. We'll try again another day." And he bowed to Beatrix, who stopped fussing about her wet paws long enough to give him a prim nod.

"But—" JR began to protest, still thinking about the disappearing strays. Another rumble interrupted him, followed by a flash of lightning. Pie squealed. "Oh, okay." He turned to Ania to offer his help if she needed it, but she'd already disappeared.

By the time they reached their row of off-white apartments, they were all soaking wet and shivering. And yet, no one seemed to mind, not even Beatrix, who was surprisingly small when her big hair was wet.

"Let's go again tomorrow!" Robert suggested as he boosted Beatrix up through her open window. "Whaddya say, Bea?"

Beatrix nodded as she scrambled inside. "If it's not too rainy, yes. I'd like to see Red Square. Boris says the Kremlin is not to be missed."

JR said nothing, not wanting to consider another outing with the embassy dogs. He headed home, wondering where all those missing strays were spending this stormy night.

11

Katerina

The rain didn't let up for days. JR sat by the window, watching the puddles grow and grow, and willing it to stop. But every time it looked like it was easing up, it only started again, harder.

He slept. He paced. He conducted thorough searches of the couch for stray crumbs. He spent an entire afternoon trying to reach a shrivelled grape under the oven with his tongue (to no avail). But it was no use. He couldn't get his mind off the Metro Dogs of Moscow—particularly the missing ones. Ania was going to try to find them, and he wanted to help her. No, he *had* to help her. Somehow.

Even walkies didn't help his restlessness. For not only was George still put out about the Dumont-Sauvage Seafaring Nomad AC III, he also hated getting his feet wet. So their walks consisted of a quick dash to the corner, where JR had to do his business while George hopped from foot to foot, trying not to let either one touch the puddles, then a quick dash home.

George could be such a cat sometimes.

He was now spending most of his evenings out with this Katerina woman. He rarely ate dinner at home, and would come tromping in late, smelling like movie popcorn or grilled meat—something far tastier than JR's old dry food. He also kept missing their eight o'clock ritual of Sleepytime tea and cookies, which annoyed JR's stomach immensely.

His only consolation was that George had yet to come home smelling like potatoes stuffed with hot dogs and bacon. That would have been too much to bear.

It was a relief when Inga the cleaning lady let herself in, pail of cleaning supplies in hand. Her visits were short, since George still hadn't unpacked, but at least she provided some distraction. JR sat on his bed and watched her whirl around the apartment, chatting to him while mopping the floor and dusting the shelves. He imagined she was saying something about the terrible weather, or some story in the news. Maybe even something about disappearing stray dogs? He sighed and rested his head on his paws. He'd never know.

On the third day of rain, right before she left the apartment, Inga noticed that the window was

still open and moved to close it. JR sat bolt upright.
A closed window would mean an end to everything
that had come to make life bearable.

A closed window was not an option.

He considered biting her, but she didn't
deserve that. So he bolted from his bed, straight
for her pail of cleaning supplies, and barrelled
right into it. It toppled over with a great clatter,
bottles spilling out left and right.

Inga shrieked and dove to save her supplies,
and within moments, she'd completely forgotten
about the window. JR returned to his bed, breathing a sigh of relief. His only punishment was a
vigorous finger-shaking, which he'd take over a
closed window any day.

Finally, on the fourth day, the rain suddenly
eased to a sprinkle, then a mist, then nothing
at all. JR pressed his nose against the glass and
squinted out at the puddles. It was over. Finally,
he could escape.

But it was mid-afternoon, and if he left now, he
might not make it back before George came home
from work. Plus, he had no idea where to find Ania

and the others during the day. No, he'd wait until George got home and left again to see Katerina. Then he'd escape. And this time, he'd go solo—no embassy dogs to horn in on his adventures.

But just then, the door swung open and George burst in, arms laden with paper grocery bags. JR leaped away from the window. George almost never came home early. What could it mean?

"I'm home early," George announced, as if that wasn't perfectly obvious. He dropped his bags on the floor and slipped off his shoes. "Good to see you, boy, but we can't go for walkies just yet."

Good to see you? JR shook his head. Had George possibly forgotten about the Dumont-Sauvage Seafaring Nomad AC III? Maybe he was sick. Maybe with some disease that erased his memory.

"Good thing I'd banked some overtime hours. I've gotta get this place in shape." George looked around, hands on his hips. "Katerina's coming for dinner."

That explained it. Only a woman could lure George home early from work *and* make him forget a prized possession. JR headed back to bed to watch the action.

Like Inga with her mop and dustpan, George whirled around the apartment, tearing open boxes and peering at the contents as if he'd never seen them before. He tossed books on the shelves and cushions on the couch, then stocked the cupboards with cans and spices. He set up the stereo and fiddled with it until he found a radio station playing something jazzy. Then he slipped an apron over his work clothes and headed for the kitchen.

"I think you'll like Katerina, buddy," George called over the sizzle of garlic on the stove. "She's beautiful—a real model, actually. Apparently, there are photos of her in Russian fashion magazines. And she's very cultured. Knows all about art."

JR yawned. George was starting to sound like Beatrix, with all her talk about culture. He wasn't falling for any of it, though. Katerina sounded just like all the others: nice, pretty, smart, and mysteriously easy for George to leave behind. He *wouldn't* get attached to her. Not this time.

Katerina arrived just as George finished assembling the salad. Tearing off his apron, he zipped to the door to meet her. JR stayed in bed. There was no point in getting the poor woman's hopes up with a warm welcome.

"So this is it," George said, sweeping his hand across the apartment. "Our humble abode." George often said ridiculous things like "humble abode" when he was trying to impress women. JR sighed. It was going to be a long night.

"Come meet my dog." George led Katerina into the living room. "This is JR."

Katerina was definitely beautiful. She was tall, even taller than George, and her dark hair reached all the way down to her waist. Her skin was snowy pale and very smooth. She probably moisturized even more often than George did.

But she was also very thin—definitely in need of a potato stuffed with hot dogs. And her dark brown eyes, though pretty, were a little intense— he didn't like how they studied him. Humans never seemed to get how unnerving it was for dogs to be stared at. He tried to stare back, but eventually, she won. He turned away, more determined than ever not to get attached to her.

Katerina crouched down and held out her hand for him to sniff. She smelled like lavender, which wasn't his favourite scent, but he let her pet his head anyway, just to be polite.

"So ..." George cleared his throat and shuffled his feet. That meant he was nervous about having Katerina in their apartment. "Nice that the rain stopped, isn't it?"

Katerina straightened and smiled at him. "Yes, it's been awful." She spoke with a strong accent, although her English was good. "But the rains bring spring, and spring is every Muscovite's favourite time of year."

"Oh yeah?" said George.

Katerina nodded. "There's nothing like the sight of green grass and flowers after a long, bitter winter. It ... it cleanses the soul. Suddenly, everyone is outside in the evenings, sitting in cafés or on park benches near the river."

She went on to describe further signs of spring, and George listened, wide-eyed, as if he'd never seen grass before. JR had just begun to doze off when she mentioned something that sounded just terrible.

Something about a dachshund.

"You have one?" asked George. Instead of being repulsed, he actually sounded impressed. JR couldn't believe it. Had he taught George nothing?

"I do. Many Muscovites do, but most of us only visit them on weekends. You'll have to come with me someday. And JR, too, of course." She glanced over at him.

JR cocked his head to one side. Muscovites loved dachshunds? But only visited them on weekends? How odd. Not that he blamed them—dachshunds were awful. Hopefully, Katerina would never bring hers to the apartment.

He made a mental note to ask Boris about this strange love of dachshunds. If anyone could explain it, Boris could.

Thankfully, George remembered that they hadn't yet gone for walkies, so before dinner, he suggested they walk to the park. Katerina, with her long legs, turned out to be a fast walker, which was a nice change from George's ambling. JR's legs were desperate for some exercise.

"Do you remember Filip Filipov, the artist?" Katerina asked George as they walked along. "He's going to launch another show at the end of this week. Very few people know about it, as usual."

"Oh yeah?" George was breathing hard from trying to keep up with Katerina. "How do you know about it?"

Katerina smiled. "I know people. This show will be different from the one you saw. It's an art show *and* a fashion show, and it will be open to the public every night for a week or two. It's called Beauty vs. Filth. Few people know it, but Filipov is actually a talented designer as well as a photographer and graphic artist." She sighed and closed her eyes. "He is a true genius."

"Yeah, he's okay, I guess," said George, who obviously wanted to be on the receiving end of Katerina's praise. "If you like that sort of thing."

Katerina opened her eyes wide. "You weren't impressed, then?"

"Oh, well, you know." George shrugged. "I just don't know if his work takes much talent."

JR snorted, picturing George at the computer, drawing moustaches on the people in his photos.

Katerina laughed. "Well, that's too bad. I was going to offer you tickets to the opening night. Only the most important people in Moscow will be there. But if you aren't impressed with his work ..."

"You've got tickets to opening night? Really?" George had ground to a halt at the sound of "the most important people in Moscow." "How'd you get them?"

Katerina smiled. "I know people," she said again. "So, you want to go?"

"Sure!" said George.

"Good. You have two tickets. You can bring a friend."

"Oh." George looked puzzled. "But what about you? Will you be there?"

She slipped her hand into the crook of George's arm. "Of course."

They passed the corner store and the owner standing outside it. "Last week, we saw a stray dog here," George told her. "He ran right inside the store and stole a ring of sausage."

Katerina nodded. "There are so many strays in Moscow. Some days, I even see them on the metro."

JR's ears pricked up. Maybe she'd seen Ania or Boris.

"On the subway? You're kidding!" George exclaimed.

"It's true," said Katerina. "They are everywhere. In fact, every few years, the city comes up with a plan to control them. Just a few days ago, I heard about another one. But there are always big protests, because some Muscovites actually like the strays."

A plan to control them! Just as Oksana, that long-haired dog at Headquarters, had said. JR held his breath, waiting for more.

"How can they like them?" asked George. "They're so dirty and sneaky."

JR bristled, and gave the leash a good, hard yank.

"Yes," said Katerina. "But they are animals. And some believe they have rights, like people."

JR couldn't tell whether she believed it herself.

"I know." JR could feel George's eyes on him. "But strays are just so ..." His voice trailed off as he searched for a word to describe them. "Oh, hey, we're here already. And look, it's John Cowley. He's the Australian Ambassador to Russia. I'll introduce you. And there's that stiff Dutch woman. Joanne something."

JR stopped at the edge of the park. Sure enough, Robert, Pie, and Beatrix were huddled together on the wet grass while their humans talked above them. Robert looked up and barked a greeting.

He froze. This was exactly what he didn't want. The dogs would definitely want to go exploring tonight, and he couldn't have them ruining his plans again.

"Come on, boy." George tugged on his leash. "Let's go see your friends."

JR followed reluctantly.

"JR!" Pie cried as he approached. "The rain stopped!"

"Oh yeah?" JR mumbled. "I hadn't noticed."

"Really?" Pie asked. "How could you not?"

"You're grumpy," Beatrix observed, which only made JR grumpier.

"I know what'll put him in a better mood," said Robert. "Another night on the town. We're all up for it. Whaddya say, J?"

JR chewed his lip. If he said no, they would just go without him. And he definitely couldn't have them out exploring with the strays while he was home alone. "Yeah, okay."

"Yahoo!" howled Robert. "Another night of freedom!"

"Shhh. Keep it down," JR said, glancing around. A Brussels griffon—small and wiry with an ugly overbite—was approaching with its human. And on the other side of the park, a lithe red dog played fetch with a tennis ball. "We can't have the whole world knowing."

"Right," Robert whispered. "Let's meet after sunset. In the back alley." His eyes gleamed.

They all agreed, then quickly changed the sub-
ject when the griffon joined them. JR could only
listen with half an ear, though, more preoccupied
with how he was going to sneak out that evening
with Katerina and George both at home.

12
The More the Merrier

"Jack Russell terriers are not the easiest dogs to raise," Katerina commented as she nibbled on her baguette.

JR stopped munching his dry food and shot her ankles a dirty look under the table. Humans weren't exactly the easiest to teach, either.

"They need a lot of exercise, don't they?"

George wiped a drop of pasta sauce from his cheek and looked over at JR. "Yeah. But he gets two walkies—I mean walks—a day."

Katerina frowned. "But he's a bit ... how do you say ... *chubby* for his size, isn't he?"

JR spat out a piece of kibble. Chubby! He was an averaged-sized Jack Russell terrier, thank you very much. No more and no less.

"Maybe a little ..." George bit his lip, and JR buried his head back in his dish. George had only just begun to offer him biscuits again—this was no time for a diet.

"Yes, I think he's a bit wider than he should be," said Katerina. He sucked in his gut. This was just too rude.

"I think he needs more walks," Katerina continued. "A third walk, in the middle of the day, would help keep off the fat."

The woman was asking for an ankle bite.

And yet ... he wouldn't say no to a midday walk ...

"Yeah, but I can't get home at lunchtime." George speared a tomato with his fork, splattering tomato juice on Katerina's blouse. She pretended not to notice.

"Well, I have a flexible schedule. Maybe I could drop by and walk him someday," she said.

"Oh!" George looked up from his pasta. He looked from Katerina to JR and back to Katerina. "Really? You'd do that? No, I couldn't ask you to do that."

Katerina nodded. "I would."

"Really?" George asked again.

JR was wondering the exact same thing. Was Katerina really that concerned about his weight? Or just trying to impress George?

He abandoned his dish and walked around the table for a better look at her. As he watched, she reached across the table and plucked a crumb off George's cheek.

Maybe she really was just a nice person. She was definitely patient with George's table manners. And generous with her event tickets.

He shook his head and returned to his food. If he didn't watch it, he'd end up liking her. He tried to focus on the fact that she had very poor taste in pets.

Thankfully, she didn't stay long after dinner, insisting she had a photo shoot the next day and needed her beauty sleep. Disappointed, George walked her to the door; if he'd been a dog, his tail would have been tucked between his legs.

JR headed to the window to make sure it hadn't started raining again. It hadn't. In fact, the sun was beginning to peek out between cracks in the clouds.

The plan for escape was still a go.

Now, the only issue was George himself. After shutting the door behind Katerina, he wandered back into the kitchen and looked at the pile of dirty dishes near the sink. Then he shrugged and headed for the couch, where he flopped down and switched on the TV to the reality show about the figure skaters.

JR sighed. The sun was sinking fast. How could he possibly escape with George right there in the living room? And supposing he couldn't get out in time? The others would assume he wasn't coming and head off by themselves. And he couldn't let that happen.

In the end, though, he didn't have to worry. Less than fifteen minutes after he'd turned on the TV, George was fast asleep in front of it, snoring like a truck. On TV, a figure skater was shouting at her partner, who had fallen on his rear end.

It wasn't an ideal situation—George could wake up at any time and notice JR's empty bed. But it would have to do. It had been four days since JR had seen Ania and the others, and who knew what had happened since then?

Not wanting to ponder the answer, he slipped out the window.

"Psst! JR! Over here!"

JR turned to see Robert and Pie peeking out from behind a garbage can in the alley.

Robert bounced out and gave himself a full-body shake. "Ready to go?"

"Ready." His legs were dying for a good run.

"Great. Us too." Robert nodded. "There's just one thing ..." He glanced back at Pie, who was slinking out from behind the garbage, looking like he'd just done a Very Bad Thing.

"Uh-oh," said JR. "What's wrong?"

"Oh, nothing's wrong. We just ..." Robert looked down at the pavement. "Well, we might have maybe invited someone else along."

"You might have maybe what?" JR squeaked, then lowered his voice. "You might have maybe *what*?"

"Actually, we might have maybe invited two someone elses along," whispered Pie, nodding back to the garbage can. Two more heads popped out from behind it. One was the little Brussels griffon they'd seen at the park earlier—the one with the ugly overbite. And the other was the thin red dog who'd been chasing balls on the grass. A vizsla, JR was fairly certain, judging by her floppy ears and how she was trembling with excitement. Vizslas were known for being ridiculously hyper.

"Meet Arne and Hazan," said Robert. "He's from Belgium, and she's from Turkey."

JR stared at them for a moment, then turned back to the brothers. "Um, guys—a word?"

They excused themselves and stepped a few feet away from the new dogs. "W-w-what were you *thinking*?" JR sputtered.

Pie ducked behind Robert, who shrugged. "Just thought it'd be fun to show some other dogs the city. The more the merrier, right?"

JR groaned. "No. Not right. Guys, this is important. We can't be bringing anyone else along!"

"Why not?" Pie whispered, peeking over Robert's shoulder.

"Why not? Because ... Because it'll ruin everything!"

"How?" asked Robert.

JR growled, then took a deep breath to calm himself. "The strays are disappearing, remember? It's a big deal, and I don't want to bother them while they're trying to figure it out."

"Well, maybe we can all help," suggested Robert.

JR cringed at the thought. "No. That's not—"

"Hey look, it's Beatrix." Robert pointed with his snout.

JR turned, and once again couldn't believe his eyes. "No *way*!" he exclaimed. For Beatrix, too, had another dog in tow—a big, tan-coloured mastiff, as tall as Ania but burly with droopy, drooly jowls. "You've *got* to be kidding me."

"Hello, everyone," Beatrix said. "This is Diego. He's from Argentina. I thought we could show him around, too."

"Hola," Diego offered in a deep, smooth voice. Hazan bounded out from behind the garbage can to give him a great big sniff, knocking over a garbage-can lid in the process. It clattered onto the pavement, and Pie leaped a good foot off the ground.

JR groaned. This had disaster written all over it. "Look, Diego ... Arne ... Hazan," he began. "I don't know what these guys told you, but you can't come. Sorry."

"Why not?" Arne narrowed his eyes at JR. He was just a hair shorter than JR, but much rounder. Obviously, a one-walkie-a-day kind of dog.

"Yeah, J." Robert turned to him. "How come?"

"There's already too many of us," JR said. "The strays don't want anyone else tagging along."

"Aw, c'mon," said Robert. "I don't think they'd mind."

"That's what they told me," JR snapped. It was only partly a lie—they had warned him not to tell the world about Kroshka Kartoshka, so he could imagine what they'd say when he showed up with an entire international contingent of embassy dogs. And it wouldn't be welcoming.

The new dogs exchanged glances, then shrugged. Slowly, they turned away and headed back down the alley. Arne glanced back over his shoulder and glared at JR.

"I don't think that was necessary." Beatrix sniffed.

"I *know* it was," JR answered, turning away from the retreating dogs and trying to ignore the feeling in his gut telling him he'd done another Very Bad Thing.

They headed for Kroshka Kartoshka, near the Arbatskaya metro. But this time, Robert barely stopped to sniff anything, and Beatrix kept quiet, only making tsking noises to herself now and then. Pie, as usual, stuck close to Robert and didn't say a word.

JR tried not to pay attention to the tension between them. He'd done the right thing. Ania and the others would have been angry if he'd brought along more dogs, and rightfully so—they would have only caused a commotion. Especially that hyper Turkish dog, whatever her name was.

Finally, after what seemed like hours of walking in silence, they were hit with the smell of stuffed potatoes. All four dogs sighed with relief.

"Oh, can we have some?" Pie pranced on the spot. "Robert, you try the Bark-and-Grab. John says your bark could wake the dead."

JR's tail drooped at the memory of his own failed attempt.

"He does say that, doesn't he?" Robert grinned, looking around. "I guess I could—"

"Look, it's them!" Beatrix cried. "The strays!"

"Oh, goody!" said Pie. "They'll have food for sure."

"You certainly changed your mind quickly," JR commented to Beatrix. "What happened to strays being filthy and flea-bitten?" It was a mean thing to say, but he couldn't help himself.

Beatrix glared at him. "They're not nearly as dirty as humans think," she said haughtily. "And they're surprisingly educated. At least, Boris is." She stretched her neck for a better view. "Is he with them?"

"Let's go see," said Robert, and they trotted off, leaving JR behind. Wishing he'd stayed home on the couch watching the fighting figure skaters, he followed.

"Hey, hey!" Robert greeted Fyodor and Ania. "Long time, no see. You guys eaten yet? We're dying for some krosh-stuff."

Fyodor and Ania were huddled together, deep in conversation. They looked up at Robert's greeting, then exchanged a quick glance.

JR slowed. Something was up, he could tell. Were they sick of the embassy dogs horning in on their food? Were they angry at *him* for bringing them again?

He ducked his head. "Guys, I'm sorry," he began. "I know you want to keep this place a secret. We'll just share a small potato, okay?"

"Forget about the potatoes," Ania snapped. JR took a step back. She was staring off into the crowd, but even more intensely than usual, as if she wanted to burn a hole right through it. She looked down at JR, then quickly looked away, but it was long enough for him to catch the sadness in her grey eyes.

He took a tentative step forward. "Is it the missing dogs again?" he asked.

Ania paused a moment, then nodded. "This time, they got Boris."

13
Spaceships, Supermodels, and Other Theories

"Boris!" Beatrix cried. "No!"

Ania pressed her lips together. "We haven't seen him for two days. And it's not like him to disappear. So, you'll excuse us for not being able to give you a tour tonight. We've got some searching to do."

"Of *course* we don't expect a tour," JR said, horrified at the thought, and at the thought of poor Boris, locked up in a cage somewhere. Or worse. "Look, let me help. I ... I don't know the city, but ... I want to help." He pictured Boris's old, scarred face and how it would light up when he talked about Russian history. They had to find him.

"We'll all help." Beatrix stepped forward.

"Count us in," Robert added.

"But what about John?" Pie whispered. His eyes were practically the size of tennis balls.

Robert looked up at the sky, which was now completely dark. "He'll be at work for another few hours at least. No worries." He turned to Beatrix. "What about your human?"

"It takes an earthquake to wake that woman," said Beatrix.

JR began to protest again, but Beatrix shot him a "don't even think about it" look. He shut his mouth and turned back to Ania.

She shook her head. "I don't think so. No offence, but we really can't afford to slow down."

"We won't slow you down!" JR protested. "I'm small but I'm fast. We're all fast," he added, although he had his doubts about Beatrix. Particularly if there were puddles.

Ania eyed him, obviously unconvinced. "Uh-huh. Look, Embassy, it's nice of you to offer, but—"

"Our mum was a first-class search and rescue dog," Robert told her. "Every time something important went missing, like a diamond ring or the TV remote, they'd call her in to find it."

Ania eyed him, too, and JR wished he had something similar to offer. Jack Russells had been bred to chase foxes and hunt down barn rats. Which was helpful, but not nearly as impressive.

Ania looked at Fyodor, who shrugged.

"Okay," she said. "I guess more eyes can't hurt." Then she glanced over at Beatrix, who was filing her nails on the sidewalk. "I guess."

"Great! Where to first?" Robert asked.

"Red Square," said Ania. "It's the last place he was seen."

"That was *amazing*!" Robert crowed as they emerged from the Ploshchad Revolutsii metro station. "I can't believe we've never taken the metro before! What a way to get around! Right, Pie? Pie?" He glanced back at his brother, who was slowly slinking up the stairs.

"Amazing," Pie wheezed. He looked like he was about to lose his dinner.

Beatrix stopped atop the stairs to smooth her whiskers. "Well," she said. "That *was* an adventure. I can't believe Johanna takes that train every day. It's *filthy*."

"But did you see those bronze statues?" Robert asked. He gave a low whistle. "This is one impressive city, Ania."

"Yeah," Ania said, studying a pair of policemen who stood nearby, eyeing people suspiciously. "It's impressive, all right. I'm not sure about its officials, though. If they're behind these disappearances ..." She shook her head.

That reminded JR of what Katerina had said. "My human's girlfriend said she heard a rumour that the city was going to control the strays," he reported. "But she said that rumour comes up every few years or so."

"It does," Ania agreed. "But we've never seen dogs disappear like this. Right?" She turned to Fyodor, who nodded. "Okay, are we all here? Where's the trembly one?"

"Here," Pie whispered, still looking dizzy.

"Let's split up and spread out around the square," said Ania. "Ask any strays you see about Boris. We'll meet back here in a few hours." She surveyed the motley group. "I'll take JR and Beatrix with me. Fyodor, you take the brothers."

Pie looked relieved not to be separated from Robert. They headed toward the State Historical Museum, a red, castle-like building capped with a white roof and turrets. It stood across the square from St. Basil's and glowed against the night sky.

"We'll head for the Kremlin," said Ania.

JR remembered Boris saying something about the Kremlin on their first trip to Red Square. He couldn't remember why, but he was pretty sure it was an important place.

"The Kremlin is where the president of Russia lives," Beatrix informed him as they wove through the crowd. "It's like a small city in itself, with cathedrals and palaces and museums inside. And it's encircled by a great wall that used to keep enemies out."

"Right," JR said, as if he already knew all this, while wishing he'd listened to Boris like Beatrix obviously had.

"Boris couldn't get enough of this place," Ania added. Her voice was scratchy, and JR looked up quickly at her. But she just looked away.

"This way," she said once they reached the huge brick wall surrounding the Kremlin. "The main gate is Oksana's territory. She might know something."

They found the long-haired blond dog that JR had first seen at Headquarters sitting near the main gate, sniffing the pockets of some guards passing by. She stood up when Ania approached, and the two exchanged a polite, if not entirely friendly, sniff.

"Well?" asked Ania.

Oksana shook her head. "No sign of him. I've barely slept these last few nights." She looked over and gave JR and Beatrix a quick once-over. She didn't seem to recognize JR, and Ania didn't bother to introduce them.

"But I'm sure you've heard the rumours," Oksana went on.

Ania nodded. "About the camps."

Oksana looked left and right, then lowered her voice. "And others, too. Like the super-model theory."

JR and Beatrix exchanged a glance. The super-model theory?

Ania sighed. "I'm not so sure about that one." She turned to JR and Beatrix. "Have you heard of Malchik?"

They shook their heads.

"Malchik was a stray who used to live at the Mendeleyevskaya station," Oksana said, sitting back on her haunches. "A very gentle dog, wouldn't even hurt a cat."

"Well, he might have hurt a cat," Ania cut in. "I mean, come on. It's a cat."

Oksana frowned and tossed her hair. "Anyway. One day Malchik was on the metro, minding his own business, and a beautiful young supermodel with a yappy little dog came on. You know the type." She looked over at Beatrix, then looked away quickly.

Beatrix gasped. "Yappy! Keeshonds are not yappy! Assertive, yes. Communicative, absolutely. But *yappy*—"

"I'm sure she didn't mean it like that," JR cut in before Beatrix could go full terrier on Oksana. She glared at him, then grumbled something nasty under her breath.

Oksana sniffed. Ania gave her a tired look.

"Anyway, the dog was barking at Malchik," Oksana continued, "so Malchik barked back. And the woman opened up her backpack, took out a knife, and stabbed him."

JR and Beatrix jumped back, as if Oksana herself had drawn a knife out of her long hair.

"Yes," Oksana said darkly. "She killed him right there on the metro. And the Muscovites were so outraged that they raised enough money to build a bronze sculpture of Malchik."

"It stands in the Mendeleyevskaya station," Ania added. "Humans rub his nose for good luck as they pass."

"Like the dog in Ploshchad Revolutsii," JR said, feeling a bit dizzy. It was one of the strangest stories he'd ever heard.

"So rumour has it that the supermodels are at it again, and that they're behind the disappearing dogs," Oksana went on. "Possibly, they want to make them into fur coats." She tossed her hair. "Which puts some of us in particular danger."

"Not with that mop, you're not," Beatrix muttered under her breath, and JR gave her a "be nice" look.

Ania scratched her ear with her hind leg. "I don't know about that theory. Boris doesn't have nice fur at all."

Oksana shrugged again. "Maybe not, but do you have a better explanation?"

Ania admitted she didn't. They thanked Oksana and moved on.

"Sounds far-fetched to me," Beatrix sniffed as they walked off.

"I hope so," said Ania.

"Me too." JR shivered at the thought of a knife-wielding supermodel.

"This way." Ania led them farther into the Kremlin grounds, along a wide street and past a white cathedral topped with gleaming gold domes. Eventually, they came to a park lined with bare trees and well-trimmed shrubs. Even in the darkness, JR could tell that it was much nicer than the park near their apartment.

"Ania!"

They all turned to see a familiar husky-type dog trotting their way.

"Sasha!" Ania called, and the relief in her voice made JR's stomach turn sour again. Why couldn't he have that effect on her?

He felt Beatrix's eyes on him and turned to see her giving him an amused look, as if she could tell just what JR was thinking. He looked away.

"You remember JR," Ania was saying to Sasha.

"Of course." The big dog nodded at him. Then he turned to Beatrix. "I don't believe we've met. I am Sasha."

"Beatrix. From the Dutch Embassy."

Sasha bowed. "Welcome to Moscow, Beatrix. I'm sorry we have to meet under such perplexing circumstances."

Beatrix nodded in return. Then she leaned over to JR and whispered, "He has very good etiquette for a stray. Handsome, too. I like him."

JR rolled his eyes.

"No sign of him, then?" Sasha asked Ania.

"Nothing. What've you heard?"

Sasha flicked an ear. "Nothing good. The control camp theory. The supermodel theory. The spaceship theory."

"The spaceship theory?" said JR. "What's that?"

"Another weird one," said Ania. "You've heard of Laika?"

Again, Beatrix and JR shook their heads.

"She was the first animal in space," said Ania. "Years ago, when the Russians and the Americans were competing to be the first humans in space, some scientists thought it would be a good idea to send up a dog first. Just in case it was too dangerous for a human." She curled her top lip. "So they found a stray. They figured that since she didn't have a human, they had a right to shoot her up to the stars. She died not long after takeoff."

"And now some dogs are worried that the disappearing strays are being sent into space," Sasha finished.

JR and Beatrix exchanged a look. The spaceship theory was even stranger and more disturbing
than the supermodel theory.

They said goodbye to Sasha and continued on,
searching the Kremlin for any sign of Boris. But
they found nothing, and no strays they met could
tell them anything they didn't already know.

Eventually, they dragged themselves back to
the Ploshchad Revolutsii metro station. Conversation had long since run out, and everyone walked
in silence, heads low to the ground.

"Any luck?" Robert came trotting up to them.

"Nothing," JR told him. "You?"

"Nothing."

"It's trouble," Fyodor grumbled, joining them.

"Yeah, it's—" Robert began, then suddenly
stopped. "Hey, wait. Where's Pie?"

"Pie?" Ania looked around. "Fyodor, where's
Pie?"

"Pie?" Fyodor repeated, turning to Robert.
"Wasn't he here a minute ago?"

"Yeah! Pie!" Robert barked, spinning in a circle.
"Pie!"

"He must be around somewhere," said Beatrix.
"Pie," she called. "Where are you?"

But an entire hour of searching couldn't turn
up any trace of Pie. No dog in Red Square had seen,
heard, or smelled the timid grey and white shepherd.

Pie, too, had disappeared.

14

Locked Up

JR awoke the following morning with a terrible feeling. The kind of feeling he always woke up with the morning after he'd done something Very Bad.

He sat up in bed and looked around, trying to remember. Sunlight was pouring through the window onto the living room floor, and George was still fast asleep on the couch, where he'd been when JR had wiggled back through the window after a long night in which he'd—

Lost Pie.

Pie was gone.

And it was all his fault.

If only, *if only* he hadn't agreed to take the embassy dogs with him in the first place. And if only, *if only* he'd just said no when they wanted to come a second time.

JR sank back onto his flannel bed, then immediately felt guilty about that, too. Wherever

Pie had slept that night, it was definitely not in a comfy flannel bed.

His only consolation was that he'd put his paw down when those new dogs had tried to come, too. Who *knew* how many of them they might have lost?

He moaned, and George stirred and looked over.

"Morning, boy," he muttered, then turned and went back to sleep.

JR had half a mind to give him a rude awakening—maybe with a sharp bark or a wet nose in his ear. But what good would it do? George couldn't bring Pie home or erase all the stupid mistakes JR had made.

He tried to go back to sleep, but all he could think about was poor Pie, peering out the window of a rocket ship as he was blasted into outer space.

It was Saturday, so George slept in. When he finally peeled himself up off the couch, it was mid-morning.

"Wow, I just conked out there, didn't I, boy? Must've been tired from all that cooking." He looked over at the pile of last night's dinner dishes next to the kitchen sink. "I'll do those later," he yawned. "How about we go exploring, boy? Maybe find a café and sit in the sun?"

Normally, the suggestion would have sent JR scrambling for his leash. But today, he could barely drag himself out of bed. The guilt about Pie weighed on him like the wool coat in Helsinki. *How* he had despised that coat.

"Hey, you sick, boy?" George knelt down to scratch his ears. "Or just lazy? Maybe Katerina's right, and you do need more walkies. Well, don't worry. We'll make this one extra long."

JR groaned. For the first time in his life, he was not up for walkies.

They found a little café not far from home and sat at an outdoor table to watch the world go by. George pretended to read a Russian newspaper while feeding JR bites of his scone. JR spat them out under the table, unable to eat anything.

Two terriers and a towering Great Dane passed by, but as hard as he searched, JR could spot no Australian shepherd with a pleasantly blank expression and a tendency to flatten himself on the pavement.

Then, on the way home, he saw a familiar grey and white shape in the park near their apartment, and for a moment, his heart leaped. But it was only Robert, out walking with a young woman.

JR tugged on the leash.

"Oh, you want to visit the park?" asked George. "Okay. Hey, isn't that one of the Aussie dogs? Where's John, though? Hey, wait!"

But JR had already yanked the leash out of George's hand and was making a beeline for the shepherd.

Robert barely looked up when he approached. His eyes were dull and his head hung low, and he admitted that he hadn't slept a wink or eaten a bite since Pie had disappeared.

"John's a wreck," Robert said. "That's why Marie's walking me today. She's his assistant," he added, nodding to the young woman at the end of his leash, who was talking to George. "John's running around posting 'Missing Dog' signs all over the Arbat. Offering a $5,000 reward for anyone who finds Pie."

JR's stomach sank. Not only had he caused terrible trouble for Pie, but he'd made Robert and John miserable, too. *What* had he been thinking?

"Wow," George remarked on their way home. "This is bad, boy. That Australian shepherd ... what was his name? Cake? Strudel? Anyway, it looks like he's been dognapped! John thinks it's because he's such a valuable purebred."

Valuable purebred! JR shook his head. If only George knew that all the other missing dogs had been anything but!

"John found an open window in their apartment. He thinks the thief just crawled right in and nabbed poor Cake." George shook his head as he opened the door to the apartment. "So he's warning everyone to make sure their windows are shut tight. And you know what? I noticed this morning that there's an open window right next to your bed."

Before JR could even process what was happening, George had marched across the apartment, pulled the window closed, and locked it.

JR sat back on his haunches, stunned. For a while, he just stared at the locked window as the meaning of it all slowly became clear. The locked window didn't just mean an end to his adventures. Adventures didn't even matter any more. What mattered was Pie, who was missing because of him. It was up to JR to find him.

And now, his only way out was locked tight.

That night, he barely slept, worrying about Pie and Boris and the missing dogs—and all the others that could disappear any day. Including Ania.

When he finally did manage to fall asleep, George came home from his date with Katerina, switched on all the lights, and searched the entire apartment for dognappers. Finally convinced that no one had sneaked in while he was out, George switched off the lights and went to bed. But JR lay awake for several hours more, wondering if every pair of feet that passed the window could belong to the human who was stealing dogs for coats or space travel ... or worse.

It was one of the longest nights of his life.

On Sunday morning, he and George were sitting on the couch—George sending emails from his laptop while JR fretted and chewed his tail—when someone buzzed their apartment.

George rose to answer it, then came back a few minutes later with Katerina on his heels.

"Wow, I ... I didn't know you were coming ... I would have ..." George glanced at himself in the mirror over the fireplace that wasn't really a fireplace and did a double take. "Excuse me for a second." He zipped into the bedroom, closed the door, and proceeded—JR could tell—to douse himself with old-fishing-boat cologne and style his hair until it looked like he hadn't really styled it at all.

That left JR and Katerina in the living room, looking at each other.

Once again, she was staring at him. *Studying* him, as if he were a pair of gloves she was considering buying.

JR looked away first, unnerved, and Katerina pulled out her handbag and began to rummage through it. As usual, she looked smashing. She wore a yellow dress under a smart blue jacket, and she had a jaunty yellow scarf tied around her neck. George had dated some very pretty women before, but Katerina was by far the most beautiful. Then again, she *was* a model. Who knew what she looked like when she rolled out of bed in the morning, before she put on her makeup and stylish clothes?

This brought to mind the supermodel theory and the story of poor old Malchik. If he ever got out of this apartment, JR decided, he would go to the Mendeleyevskaya station and see Malchik's statue. It would only be right to pay his respects.

Something flashed on the edge of his vision, and he looked back at Katerina.

And practically jumped out of his fur.

Katerina had a knife.

JR leaped off the couch and scrabbled across the floor to the bedroom. He shoved open the door with his head, then zipped in and dove under the bed.

"Hey!" George exclaimed from inside the sweater he was pulling over his head. "What's going on? JR?" He marched out of the room, exchanged some muffled words with Katerina, then came back and knelt down on the floor.

"What's the matter with you, boy? Katerina said you went crazy when you saw her pocket knife. Is that it? She was just cutting a loose thread off her jacket. Come out. It's okay."

Cutting off a thread. JR let out his breath. Just cutting off a thread. Nothing to be scared of.

But the image of Katerina in her yellow dress wielding a small but very sharp-looking knife flashed through his brain. He couldn't move.

"Since when have you been afraid of pocket knives?" George asked. "You old scaredy-cat."

Scaredy-cat! If JR could have spoken Human, he would have said something along the lines of "Since you moved us to a city with killer supermodels, stupid." But as it was, he had no choice but to come out and try to act dignified. There was nothing worse than being called a scaredy-cat.

Still trembling, he inched toward George's outstretched hand.

"There. That's better." George stroked his head with his warm, well-moisturized hand, then scooped him up under one arm. He carried him like a football back to the living room.

So much for dignity.

Once everything was back to normal, Katerina announced her purpose for coming: to make them a hearty Russian breakfast. She set to work whipping up some *blini,* which JR knew, thanks to Boris, meant pancakes. She chatted to George over her shoulder as she measured and stirred ingredients together, and JR had just begun to breathe normally again when she brought up her dachshund.

"I plan to go next weekend," she told him. "Would you like to come? You can bring JR. I think he'd love it."

JR sighed. Just when he was beginning to get used to her, she had to remind him about the dachshund. Hopefully George already had plans for next weekend.

"Next weekend? Sure!" said George. "That sounds like a great time to visit."

Is there ever a good time to visit a dachshund? JR wondered. He couldn't think of one.

"It's about an hour out of the city," Katerina said over the sizzle of *blini* in the frying pan. "And it needs some work."

They all do, thought JR. For one thing, they need real legs.

"For one thing, it needs a new coat of paint," said Katerina, sliding a paper-thin pancake out of the pan and onto a plate.

Paint?

"And the plumbing is a bit of a mess."

The dachshund's plumbing was a mess? Either this was one unfortunate dog, or Katerina was talking about something else completely.

"Summer houses must be pretty affordable around here, if so many Muscovites have them," said George, accepting the stack of pancakes she placed before him.

Summer house?

"Yes." Katerina pulled a container of sour cream out of the fridge and set it in front of George, gesturing for him to spread it on his *blini*. "And they're also just an important part of the culture. We take great pride in our *dachas*. They are—how do you say—like little refuges away from the city."

JR cocked his head to one side. Had she actually said dachshund? Or something else? He listened hard.

"Well"—George dumped a glob of sour cream on his pancake—"I'm excited to see this *dacha*."

JR sighed with relief. They were saying *dacha*, not dachshund. Which apparently meant a summer house, not a weiner dog. What a relief.

Katerina dropped half a pancake in JR's dish, and he dashed over to gobble it up.

Delicious.

Now the conversation made much more sense. It was even exciting—the next weekend, they'd pack up her little car and drive out to the country to her *dacha*. George would *have* to let him off-leash. And there would *have* to be squeaky things to chase—no summer house would be complete without them.

JR stretched out in a sunbeam under the table, allowing himself, just for a little while, to forget about the missing dogs of Moscow. But soon, the sun ducked behind a cloud and they barged right back into his brain, filling his belly once again with guilt and dread.

Then something miraculous happened. George got up to go to the washroom, and after a moment, Katerina stood up, too. She looked around, then darted to the window. And as JR watched, incredulous, she unlatched it and opened it—not wide, but just a crack.

Just enough. JR could do the rest.

He stared at her as she returned to the table and rearranged her napkin on her lap. Why on earth had she done it?

And then it occurred to him. Katerina didn't care for the old-fishing-boat cologne any more than Inga did! She'd opened the window to air the place out.

For once, he was completely, utterly thankful for George's awful taste in cologne.

15

A Second Look

Not long after breakfast, someone else buzzed their apartment.

"Now who could that be?" George wondered, rising from the table. He headed for the door, then returned several minutes later, frowning.

"So, remember that missing dog I told you about? The Australian ambassador's dog?" he asked Katerina.

She nodded.

"Well, John—he's the ambassador—has decided to have some kind of a memorial for him at the park, and apparently, it's starting right away. That was his assistant, Marie, at the door." George shrugged. "It's not a funeral or anything— John's still trying hard to find poor old Quiche. It's a ceremony to honour him, I guess." He looked down at JR, then back at Katerina. "Sorry about this. I'm sure you won't want to come—"

"Oh, I'll come," Katerina said quickly. "I'd like to."

They stacked the dishes and headed for the park, where a small crowd was already gathering near one of the skinny, leafless trees. Robert, John, and Marie were there, of course. And so were Beatrix and Johanna. But there were other dogs, too—JR cringed when he saw the three who'd wanted to come along on the last outing. The big Argentinian mastiff nodded at him, but the little Brussels griffon with the overbite shot him a nasty look.

John was in rough shape. His eyes were bloodshot and his hair tangled, and he couldn't speak without his voice catching in his throat. He said a few words about Pie's loyalty and good nature, then pulled a small statue of a shepherd dog out of a bag and placed it at the base of the tree. JR couldn't help noting that it looked more like a German shepherd than an Australian shepherd, but he kept that to himself.

After the ceremony had ended, George bent his head toward Katerina. "John looks awful, doesn't he?" he said.

Katerina looked John up and down. "He looks like he got dressed in the dark. Black pants with brown shoes?" She tsked.

George nodded sadly. "Maybe I should offer to take him out. You know, to get his mind off Crumble."

Katerina tucked her arm through George's. "That's a nice idea."

"I know!" George snapped his fingers. "I'll give him the extra ticket to the Filip Filipov show you gave me the other day."

Katerina frowned. "I'm not sure that's a good idea."

"Why not?" asked George. "I know he's not very fashionable, but I bet he'd enjoy it."

She looked doubtful. "I think everyone there will be much younger ..."

"Ah, John's not that old. I bet he'd—"

"What's this about John's age?" John himself appeared at George's shoulder, startling both him and Katerina.

"Um, we were just talking about an art show." George took his wallet out of his back pocket and pulled out the tickets. "Opening night is at eight o'clock tomorrow. Wanna come?"

John stared at the tickets. "That's ... that's kind of you," he snuffled. "But I don't know ..." He glanced down at the statue of the German shepherd, then pulled a handkerchief out of his pocket and gave his nose a honk.

Katerina smothered her grimace with a well-manicured hand.

"You'll like it," George promised. "Filip Filipov is a genius, and this particular show will showcase both his fashion and photography. It's called Beauty and Filth."

"Beauty *versus* Filth," Katerina corrected him, looking down at John's rumpled trousers. It wasn't hard to guess which one she thought best described the Australian ambassador.

George pondered this. "Like a competition?"

Katerina looked impatient. "It's a statement about society."

George shrugged and turned back to John. "Anyway, only the most important people in Moscow have tickets to opening night."

"I *have* heard a lot about this Filipov guy," John said, swallowing hard. "And maybe I could use a break from ..." He glanced at the statue again and sighed. "All right. I'll go."

"Great." George patted Katerina's arm. "It's at 460 Petrovsky. We can go together."

"JR!"

Beatrix was headed his way, pulling Johanna behind her. Even Beatrix looked a bit dishevelled close up, with a straggle of grey hair hanging in her eyes. In all the commotion, Johanna must have forgotten about her daily grooming.

"I've been thinking," she began before he could say anything. "There has to be another way out of our apartments, and we need to find it and get back out. Tonight. What about—"

The thought of the embassy dogs joining him again made JR shudder. When he went back out, it would be alone. And this time, he meant it. "I don't know, Beatrix," he said.

"What do you mean, you don't know?" Beatrix snapped. "Boris and Pie are missing, and—" She stopped, then gave him a steely look. "You're planning to go out by yourself, aren't you?"

"Me? No." JR looked away.

"You are." Beatrix huffed her hair out of her eyes. "Well, that's just *fine.* Go on by yourself, and good luck." She turned to go, then whirled back around. "But let me tell you something," she said. "You go on and on about your human needing to have adventures by himself, and being unable to let someone into his life."

"I don't—" JR began, but she shook her big head.

"But what you don't realize is, you're just like him!"

And she turned and stomped off, once again yanking Johanna behind her.

"Ania!"

JR wove through the crowd toward her, the sight of her long, golden ears filling his belly with warmth, like the sound of George's keys in the door after a long day As soon as George and Katerina had left that evening—this time to some dinner party in the suburbs—he'd escaped out the window, which thankfully George hadn't noticed was open. He'd headed straight for Kroshka Kartoshka near the Arbatskaya, praying she'd be there. And sure enough, she was.

Ania looked at him for a moment as if she couldn't quite place him, then blinked. "Embassy. Hi. I didn't expect to see you. Where are the others?"

Her eyelids were drooping and her grey eyes were dull. He'd never seen her look so ... defeated.

"They're all at home," JR told her. "When Pie disappeared, his human decided he must have been dognapped, and he told all our humans to lock their windows. I only got out because my human's girlfriend opened ours, and my human didn't notice."

He felt a sudden rush of guilt, remembering how Beatrix had wanted to come, too. But then he recalled the other thing she said, and the back of his neck burned. Just like George! He definitely was *not*. George left behind perfectly nice and good people who cared about him. JR just wanted to leave behind some annoying embassy dogs who'd slow him down and ...

He shook himself, not wanting to think about it.

"Oh," Ania said in a flat voice. "That's good." A skinny teenaged boy passed by, balancing a box of Kroshka Kartoshka on top of a pile of school books. "Easy pickings," Fyodor would have called him. But Ania barely gave him a glance.

"Hey, you want to know something funny?" JR asked, hoping to see some life in her eyes. "Pie's human is convinced that Pie was dognapped because he's a purebred."

Ania didn't laugh, but the corners of her mouth twitched a little. "That is kind of funny," she admitted.

It wasn't much, but JR was encouraged. "So where's Fyodor?" he asked.

"Headquarters," Ania said. "That's where they're all staying now. It's the only place we know for sure is safe."

"Oh." JR eyed her ribs. He could count every one, despite the fur that covered them. "Are you hungry?"

She shook her head. "I can't eat. I can't do anything, really, except keep searching. But ..." She lowered her head to his level. "To be honest, I'm starting to lose hope. I've been searching all day, every day. Sometimes all night, too. And still, there's no sign of Boris or Sergei. Or Pie."

"I'll look with you," he said quickly. "My human's gone out to the suburbs for the evening. He'll get stuck in traffic for sure and won't be back for hours."

This time, Ania hesitated only a moment before agreeing, and his belly felt warm again. They left Kroshka Kartoshka and took a side street, which apparently had no rules for parking, judging by the cars that had been abandoned every which way. They began to check under and around each one for some sign of the missing dogs.

Maybe it was the fact that neither Fyodor nor Sasha was around. Or maybe it was just the nature of the situation. But that night, for the first time, Ania seemed to want to talk. As they searched, she asked about his human and how he managed to keep sneaking out. He told her all about Katerina, too. Then, in another attempt to make her laugh, he told her the story of Katerina's pocket knife, omitting the part about being a scaredy-cat. And this time, it actually worked. Ania let out a real laugh— the first he'd ever heard from her. The warmth spread from his belly out to his nose and his tail.

Then suddenly she stopped, staring at something above her on a lamppost. It was a sign, and although JR couldn't read English, let alone Russian, he knew right away that the big bold letters said something to the effect of "Missing Dog." For there, underneath them, was a photo of Pie, looking at the camera as if it might bite him.

The warmth disappeared, and he shivered. They moved on without a word.

They searched alleys and doorsteps. They looked behind dumpsters and garbage bins. They checked every corner of every underpass they could find, calling the names of every stray Ania knew had disappeared. But hours later, they still hadn't found any sign of the dogs.

"Let's take a break," JR suggested, wondering how Ania was managing to stay standing with no sleep and no food. His belly was already grumbling and his legs ached. "Just for a little bit. Let's sit and think about what to do next."

Ania sighed. "All right." She looked around. "Over there?" She pointed with her snout toward a bank whose wall had been covered in some kind of brightly coloured mural. In fact, it looked like a Filip Filipov piece—a big splash of colour in a most unlikely place.

Sure enough, when they drew closer, they saw the signature double *F*'s on the giant poster glued to the wall. A few people were standing in front of it, studying it intently.

Ania and JR joined them, sitting down on their haunches. At first glance, it looked like a picture of St. Basil's Cathedral, with all its colourful domes and spires. But on closer examination, it became clear that Filipov had actually taken hundreds, even thousands of tiny photos and stitched them together to make the shape of St. Basil's.

It was remarkable, really. If JR squinted hard enough, he could make out little images of children, trains, buildings, cows, churches, and even dogs. But eventually, staring at it made his head hurt, and Ania seemed to feel the same way. They stood up and wandered off.

"Where will you go now?" he asked when his stomach told him it was long past eight o'clock— time to head home.

She flicked a bug off her ear. "I don't know. Headquarters, I guess. The last thing I want to do is give in and admit they've beaten us, whoever 'they' are. But ..." She hung her head. "What choice do I have?"

He couldn't think of an answer to that—there was no way George would overlook a towering golden dog in their apartment.

"See you around, Embassy," Ania said. And she turned and slipped away into the crowd.

16
A Surprise Visit

JR spent most of the next day pacing the kitchen. By late afternoon, he'd lost track of how many times he'd circled the table, and was no closer to solving the mystery of the missing dogs.

He circled again. The pacing was also helping to keep his mind off the fact that he had to do his business, *very* badly. George had said he'd be late getting home, and late he was. JR didn't need a clock to tell him that they ought to have been halfway to the park by now.

A shadow at the window caught his eye, and he paused. For a moment, he saw nothing, but then it moved again—a big, dark shadow. Instinct kicked in, and before he knew it, he was at the window, barking his head off.

"JR!" Katerina's face appeared, and he jumped. Her long hair was pinned up on her head, and she wore a smart blue skirt, a white blouse, and high heels. "Good dog," she said, as if there was nothing strange about her appearing at the window. "No barking, now."

Katerina pulled the window open as wide as it would go, and slipped her briefcase through. Then, as JR watched in utter confusion, she proceeded to squeeze *herself* through the open window.

He took several steps back. This was very, very strange. He was fairly certain that humans were supposed to enter apartments through doors. And moreover, that they really shouldn't be skinny enough to squeeze through open windows. Katerina was *seriously* in need of a stuffed potato.

Inside, she stood up and dusted herself off. "There," she said. "Now come, JR. We're going for a walk."

JR had forgotten about her offer to drop by and walk him. It had sounded like a good idea at the time, but now, somehow, it just didn't feel right.

She folded her long arms over her chest and studied him for a moment. Then she nodded. "You're perfect, you know that? Ideal."

JR cocked his head in surprise. It was nice of her to notice of course, but still.

"Yes, it will be very interesting to see how you do," Katerina continued. "Now go get your leash."

Now he was thoroughly confused. To see how he'd do? This was a *very* strange situation indeed.

"Go on," she commanded, picking her briefcase up off the floor. But the handle chose that moment to snap right off, and the briefcase slipped out of her hands and back onto the floor. Papers spilled everywhere, and Katerina cursed.

Thick, glossy pages rained down around JR, and he paused to look at them. They were fashion photos, which wasn't surprising, considering Katerina's line of work. What *was* surprising was the scenes they depicted. In one, a woman stood in a dirty alley wearing a tattered black dress. She had very dark makeup and her hair was matted, as if she hadn't combed it in years. Kind of like Boris's.

It took JR a moment to realize that the woman in the photo was Katerina.

He looked up at her, then back to the photo. Why on earth would she dress like this? Another picture had her in a stained suit with ripped sleeves, leaning on a dumpster. Yet another showed her sitting in a gutter next to a skinny spotted dog, obviously a—

Stray.

JR froze as an utterly crazy idea came to him.

"JR." Katerina looked up from the photos she was gathering. "What are you doing? I told you to go get your leash."

He ignored her, pushing some photos around with his nose until he found one that interested him. It showed another tattered model in an underground parking lot, petting a confused-looking retriever.

His heart now firmly lodged in his throat, he searched again, flinging pages aside with his teeth until he found the one he was looking for. When he saw it, his stomach turned a flip.

A tall, blond woman wearing what looked to be a burlap bag stood in the middle of a busy street, ignoring the traffic around her to stare at the camera. At her side stood a big, brown dog.

A big, brown dog with a familiar scar over his right eye.

JR dragged his eyes away from Boris to the bottom right-hand corner of the image, where the photographer had left a stamp.

Double *F*'s, placed back to back.

His stomach flipped again. Katerina worked for Filip Filipov.

And Filip Filipov had the missing stray dogs.

"JR," Katerina repeated, this time loud and sharp. "Get the leash." He looked up into her dark eyes. The corner of her lip twitched. "There's no time to waste," she added, taking a step toward him.

Looking back, JR wasn't sure whether he'd jumped out the window before or after he realized that Katerina was about to dognap him. Not that it mattered. He was outside on the pavement before she could stop him.

"J-Aaaarrrrrrrrrr!"

Katerina had a surprisingly loud scream. She was also surprisingly quick when it came to wriggling out windows. And she could run surprisingly fast, too, especially considering that she was wearing high heels.

JR sprinted down the street, hung a right, then zipped up the next, but Katerina stayed close behind. She was cursing in Russian—JR recognized some of the words the skinny man with the sunglasses had uttered when the strays stole his dinner.

Oh, *where* were the strays when JR needed them?

He glanced over his shoulder. Was she actually *gaining* on him? He kicked it into high gear and sprinted for the park, hoping her high heels would sink like pegs into the mud.

The embassy dogs out walking in the park stopped and stared when they saw him coming.

"JR!" Beatrix cried. "What's going on?"

"Are we racing?" Hazan the Turkish vizsla abandoned the ball she was chasing and bounded toward JR. "I love racing!"

"Who's the crazy woman?" yelled Robert.

"Amigo!" Diego the Argentinian mastiff called. "Are you in trouble?"

For the first time, JR was actually glad to see them.

"Can't stop!" he panted as he zipped past. "Crazy supermodel!"

Moments later, Katerina shrieked, and he glanced back, hoping her heels had gotten stuck in the grass. But what he saw made his mouth fall open. He dug his nails into the dirt to stop himself.

The dogs must have all yanked their leashes away from their humans, for they were now running in tight circles around Katerina's long legs. She was screaming at the top of her lungs, turning and turning, looking for a way out. But it was no use. The dogs were zipping around her so fast that within moments, she was so dizzy she toppled over onto the grass.

Cheering, the embassy dogs sprinted for JR while their humans dove to help Katerina.

"Wow!" was all JR could say as they gathered around him. "That was amazing!" In fact, it was the most impressive rescue he'd ever seen. Even better than the time the strays had saved him from the crazy man.

"What's going on?" asked Arne, the Brussels griffon.

JR took a deep breath. "I ... I know where the strays are. Pie, too," he added, and Robert's eyes grew wide. "At least, I know who has them. I don't know how to find him, or how to save them, but ..." Actually, now that he thought of it, he had no idea what to do next.

"We're coming," Robert said without hesitation.

"Absolutely," Beatrix agreed.

JR glanced over at Katerina, who was picking herself off the ground. A few humans were marching toward them, calling their names. Then he looked back at the embassy dogs, who were all watching him expectantly. They had gone and rescued him, even though he hadn't let them come along to explore the city. He'd been selfish. He'd been heartless. He'd been—

George.

He looked up at Beatrix, who was giving him a knowing look. "Later," she said. "Right now, we have other things to worry about." She nodded at the approaching humans.

"Don't even try to leave us behind," warned Arne.

"La unión hace la fuerza," said Diego. They all turned to him, and he translated, "Strength in numbers."

JR looked back at Katerina, remembering the impressive rescue. Diego was right. And although it was sure to be chaos, he *wanted* them to come.

"Let's go!" he cried. "Now!"

Robert let out a whoop, and they all took off sprinting, shoulder to shoulder, without even a backward glance at their bewildered humans.

17
460 Petrovsky

Once they were sure they'd outrun their humans, the embassy dogs stopped to make a plan. Arne immediately set to work unfastening everyone's leash.

"Sometimes the overbite comes in handy," he said, springing open the clasp on Robert's leash with his teeth.

"Thanks, Arne!" Robert cried, giving himself a whole-body shake. "Okay, J, tell us everything."

JR took a breath, then proceeded to tell them all about Katerina, her surprise entrance, and the contents of her briefcase.

"So *Filip Filipov* has the missing dogs?" Beatrix exclaimed when he was done.

"Who's Filip Filipov?" asked Hazan.

"Only one of the most famous artists in Moscow today!" Beatrix told her. "He shows his work wherever he wants—on buildings, bus shelters, anywhere. His work is very contemporary," she added. "I don't care for it much."

"Anyway," said JR, "I'm pretty sure Filipov has the missing strays. And he's opening a new show tonight. It's kind of a secret—apparently only important people are invited. And I don't know if the dogs will be there, but it's worth a shot." He closed his eyes, trying to remember Katerina's conversation with George and John the day before. "I'm pretty sure I remember the address, but I don't know how to find it."

Robert sighed. "Can't help you there."

Arne unfastened Diego's leash and shook his head. "Me neither."

"We need the strays," Beatrix declared. "They know everything about the city."

JR nodded. He'd been thinking the same thing.

"Where should we look for them?" asked Diego.

JR chewed on his lip. "I think I know. I just hope I can find it." He took a deep breath. "Who's up for a ride on the metro?"

"Move over!" Arne hissed.

"I can't!" Hazan yelped, nodding at Beatrix. "She's taking up all the room!"

Beatrix turned and glared at them. "There's a puddle on my other side," she growled. "I'm *not* moving over."As the train rumbled and shifted on the tracks underneath them, Hazan whined. The human standing next to her finished eating his candy bar and dropped the wrapper on the floor. Hazan pounced on it, swallowing the wrapper in one gulp. Arne made a face.

Robert sat next to JR, panting hard. "It's stuffy as the outback in December in here," he said. "And I don't remember it being so busy last time."

JR agreed. This time, the train was packed with humans heading home from work. Every seat was taken, and many people were standing shoulder to shoulder, clutching handles that hung from a pole overhead. "This must be what they call rush hour."

"Ow!" Robert winced as someone stepped on his tail. "Think I'd rather walk."

"Would you move over?" Arne said again.

"I told you, I can't!" Hazan wailed. Then she moaned. "Ohh, I shouldn't have eaten that wrapper."

JR tried hard to concentrate on the announcer's voice. It was a female voice, so he knew they were headed the right way, away from the centre of town. He even thought he recognized the names of a few stops.

The train curved around a corner and Arne lost his balance, stepping on Hazan's paw. She yipped and startled Beatrix, who bared her teeth and snapped back. But JR stayed upright, bending his knees and moving with the train. Riding the metro didn't seem quite as strange any more. In fact, he realized, getting around the city this way was starting to feel almost natural.

"Mayakovskaya station," said the announcer.

"That's us!" he told the others, letting the crowd of humans sweep him out the doors and onto the pink marble floor. He chose the hall he was fairly certain Sasha had led them down, and got Diego to shove open the black door at the end of it. Then he took them down a staircase and along another corridor until finally he saw the heavy wooden door he was looking for. Relieved, he lifted a paw and scratched the door twice, paused, then scratched again. Just as Sasha had done.

At first, no one answered. He waited, then scratched again.

Nothing.

Just as he was starting to panic, someone called, "Who's there?"

"Um, JR."

A pause. Then, "Who?"

"JR," he said, louder this time. "I'm a friend of Ania's. I've got some news about—"

"Password?"

"Um," JR closed his eyes, trying to remember. *"Bez ... Bezdomnaya sobaka?"*

The door opened and a small grey head peered around it, eyes beady and suspicious. It was the adorable but vicious terrier.

She gave each of the embassy dogs a once-over. "And these are?" She glared at them.

"Friends," said JR. "Please, if you'll just let us in, I've got news. I ... I know where the missing dogs are."

The terrier looked him up and down, eyes narrowed. She glanced over her shoulder, then said, "Come in."

They walked into the fancy old room, which, as JR had expected, was full of stray dogs on couches. Robert let out a low whistle.

"Oh my," whispered Beatrix. "*Look* at that chandelier."

"Hazan, don't break anything," Arne warned.

"I'll try," whimpered Hazan, her rear end trembling.

"Embassy!" Ania leaped off one of the couches. "What are you doing here?"

"Ania!" he cried. "I figured it out! I know where the missing dogs are!"

All at once, they were surrounded by strays.

"What do you mean you know?" Fyodor demanded.

"Did you see them? Where are they?" Sasha pushed his way to the front of the crowd.

"Let him talk!" Ania commanded. "JR, who took them?"

JR took a deep breath and looked around. "Filip Filipov."

Silence followed. After a few moments, Fyodor repeated, "Filip Filipov?"

"The artist?" Sasha cocked his head to the side.

"Why would he want stray dogs?" the dim-looking retriever wondered.

"I know it sounds crazy." JR turned to Ania. "But you've just got to believe me. I saw them in his pictures. I swear. In fact," he added as another thought came to mind, "I bet they were in that big poster we saw last night! Remember? The one on the side of the bank?"

"JR is an honest and noble dog," Diego put in. "He wouldn't lie."

"Thanks," JR whispered. "I wouldn't," he added to Ania.

"Okay," said Ania, but her voice was thick with doubt. "If you say so. But where are we going to find him?"

"He never comes out in public, you know," said Sasha.

"I know," said JR. "But he has a show tonight. And ... and I don't know for sure that the dogs will be there. But I'm going to go see."

"And so are we," added Beatrix, stepping up beside him.

"All of us," added Arne.

"You don't have to believe me," said JR. "But I need you to tell me how to find 460 Petrovsky. That's where the show is."

Sasha shook his head. "It can't be there. There are only warehouses on that street."

JR frowned. He was fairly certain that was the address Katerina had given.

Ania stared hard at him for a moment, then looked around at the other metro dogs. "Well then, I'll go, too," she said.

"Ania, no." Sasha stepped toward her. "It's not safe. We can't leave." He turned to JR. "I know you mean well, but you're on your own. I'm sorry."

JR's tail drooped. Then he remembered something important. "Well, you're wrong about one thing," he told Sasha. "I'm not on my own." He looked back at the embassy dogs, who nodded and squared their shoulders.

"You're wrong about another thing, too," Ania added. "I'm going."

"Ania!" Sasha said sharply, but she shook her head.

"I'd rather try than stay here and wait for them to find us." She looked down at JR. "If JR thinks Filipov has the dogs, I have to go."

JR's tail sprang back up. She trusted him. Now, hopefully, he'd be able to prove his theory right.

"Well, I'm not staying here," said Fyodor.

"Me neither," said the adorable but vicious one. "If Filipov really is the dognapper, well ..." She held up a paw and flashed some surprisingly sharp claws.

"He won't know what bit him," Fyodor concluded.

In the end, a dozen strays joined the six embassy dogs on the metro, bound for 460 Petrovsky. The train heading back into the centre of town wasn't nearly as busy as the one going out, which was a good thing, since eighteen dogs took up an awful lot of space. In fact, they took up an entire car of their own, much to the bewilderment of the human passengers.

"Move along, move along," Fyodor said as a woman stumbled down the aisle, trying to avoid stepping on legs and tails. "This car's for the canines, lady."

The dogs chuckled.

Ania, however, wasn't laughing. "What time is the show?" she asked JR.

"Eight o'clock," he said. He tuned in to his stomach. "About an hour from now."

She nodded. "I hope this works."

JR swallowed hard. He hoped so, too.

Four-sixty Petrovsky was indeed in the middle of an industrial area. The street was lined on either side with ugly brown warehouses. Many had cracked windows, and JR could smell the rats inside from half a block away. If it hadn't been for the long line of humans in front of one building, he would have assumed he had the wrong address.

"That must be it," Beatrix said as they watched the crowd from across the street. "Those people look important. Look how they're dressed. All those suits and fancy shoes."

She was right. Which made it all the more strange to see them queuing in front of a decrepit warehouse.

"Okay, we've got to split up," said Ania. "Eighteen dogs can't just barge in there together. I'll take a group, and Fyodor, you'll take another. JR, you'll take one, too."

JR gulped. He'd been hoping to just follow Ania's lead. But he nodded, and the embassy dogs clustered around him, claiming him for their leader. That made him feel stronger.

"Fyodor, you go first. Try to find a way inside, but make sure they don't spot you," Ania instructed.

Fyodor nodded and led his group toward the building, keeping a good distance from the crowd. JR watched them, amazed at how they managed to slink along, practically blending into the street. He stole a glance at his own group—from big-haired Beatrix to hyperactive Hazan. If they managed not to draw the humans' attention, it would be a miracle.

"Look!" Ania hissed. "They've found a door. They're in."

Sure enough, the dogs were disappearing into the warehouse through a side door. Fyodor glanced back at them, winked, and slipped into the building. No one in line appeared to notice.

"Okay, JR. Wait a few minutes, then take your team in there, too," said Ania.

"Okay," JR whispered. "Ready guys?"

"Ready!" said Robert.

"Ready!" said Diego.

Hazan whined and pranced on the spot.

"Hazan, you've got to stay calm," JR told her.

"I'll try," she whimpered. "It's just all so exciting."

He sighed. "Okay, come on."

To reach the side door, they had to approach the humans, close enough to hear their conversations. Most were speaking Russian, of course, but JR's ears picked up a bit of English. He listened hard.

"Beauty vs. Filth is supposed to be the greatest art show of the year," a woman was saying. "I think it's brilliant of Filipov to make a statement about society through fashion."

"Oh yeah?" said the man next to her. "What's he trying to say?"

JR stopped. He knew that voice. And ... He sniffed. Leather with a hint of cinnamon. He looked up, and sure enough, there was George, standing in line with John Cowley, chatting with the woman beside them.

What had George done, he wondered, when he'd come home and found JR gone? Katerina must have cooked up some kind of excuse. Otherwise, surely he wouldn't be here, chatting as if nothing were amiss.

"Why are we stopping?" Arne hissed, and JR shook himself.

"Sorry," he whispered. "That's my human."

"And mine next to his," added Robert. "Come on, keep going. If they see us, we're done for."

They made a dash for the side door and slipped inside. Within seconds, they were all blinking in the dim light of the warehouse.

18

Beauty vs. Filth

The warehouse was a maze of narrow corridors and rooms separated by thin walls and canvas curtains. A few flickering bulbs overhead provided the only light, and the air was chilly—much colder than outside.

JR chose a corridor and led the others down it, trying to stay as quiet as possible. The dogs behind him did the same—the only noise was the click of their nails on the concrete floor and some distant, thumping music. They peered into the first room on their right, but found it empty. The next room, on their left, was filled with boxes.

The third room, however, was a little more interesting. It held stacks of huge framed images, and what with their bright colours and strange mishmash of people and landscapes, JR could tell they were the work of Filip Filipov.

"Do you think this is his studio?" Arne whispered, peering around JR's shoulder.

"Maybe."

"These photos must be worth a lot of money," Beatrix pointed out. "I'm sure those humans outside would love to get their hands on them."

They moved on. At the end of the corridor, they turned left and searched two more rooms, but found neither missing dogs nor any clues that might lead to them. The thumping music was growing louder now.

"We must be getting close to the show," said Robert.

JR stopped and listened. There were voices, too—the humans were probably filing inside, taking their seats.

"There must be a big room over there." He pointed with his snout in the direction of the voices and music. "Let's head that way."

They found another corridor leading in that direction and turned down it, just in time to see a short, stout man marching toward them.

"Back! Go back!" JR hissed, turning tail and sprinting back the way they'd come. They dove into a room full of paint cans and huddled in the darkness until the man's footsteps passed.

JR let out his breath. "That was close." He led the others back out, toward the music again.

They hadn't gone ten steps, though, when once again, they heard humans—this time, voices. And very close by. The dogs flattened themselves against the wall to listen. The voices were coming from the room on the other side. JR motioned for the others to stay back while he crept up to the door to investigate.

Slowly, carefully, he peered inside. Several humans were hurrying around, talking loudly over the music. He wasn't sure exactly what they were saying, but he could tell they were getting ready to go onstage. Three of them were obviously models, although he wouldn't have known it if he hadn't seen Katerina's photos. Their clothes were tattered and ragged, barely clothes at all, and their faces were caked with purple and black makeup. They looked so terrible that JR had half a mind to turn and run. But he forced himself to stay put.

A door on the other side of the room opened, and in marched the short, stout man who'd passed them minutes before. JR gasped. The man held the leashes of two muzzled dogs—one stocky black hound with white freckles on his snout, and one Australian shepherd with a pleasantly blank expression.

Sergei and Pie.

As JR watched, the man walked the dogs over to a woman who was painting one of the model's eyelids dark blue. She abandoned the model, crouched down in front of the dogs, then motioned for the man to bring her a bucket full of dirt that sat nearby. He obeyed, then left, and the makeup artist proceeded to dust Sergei with dirt.

JR watched in bewilderment. Why, he wondered, wasn't she dusting Pie as well? Was Pie the beauty to Sergei's filth? That didn't seem fair. Sergei was smart and kind and not bad looking as far as strays went. And then, what about the "versus" part of the show's title? Where did the competition come in?

The man returned, this time dragging a big, steel-grey dog with a heavy choke chain around his neck and a giant muzzle over his mouth. He was as tall as Ania and as broad as Diego. And judging by the way he was snarling and snapping, he was angry. *Very* angry.

The makeup artist kept her distance as she tossed dirt in the grey dog's face, too. He growled and lunged for her, but the man held fast to his leash. At one point, the man tried to make him sit, and when the big dog refused, the man kicked his legs out from under him. The dog roared, only to receive another faceful of dirt.

JR couldn't believe it. Why on earth were they provoking him like that? All the grey dog needed was a calm hand and a few comforting words. It was almost as if they were *trying* to make him angry. Almost as if ...

"Oh no," he whispered as the pieces fell into place. "Beauty *versus* filth."

He turned and raced back to his crew.

"They're in there," he reported. "Sergei and Pie. It looks like they're part of the show."

"Pie's there?" Robert yelped, then looked around and lowered his voice. "Is he okay?"

"I think so," JR said, choosing not to mention the muzzle. "For now. But there was another dog in there, a big, angry one. And I'm not sure, but I have a feeling there's going to be a fight."

"Well, surely the humans will stop it." said Beatrix.

JR shook his head. "I think it's part of the show."

"A dog fight?" Hazan squealed.

"Maybe," said JR. "I've just got this feeling ..."

"We need to get them out. Now," said Robert.

"What do we do?" asked Beatrix.

"I don't know, I—" JR began, then froze, hearing more footsteps. This time, they were coming from behind them. "More humans. Go!"

They scampered down the corridor, toward the thumping music. But this time, they weren't quite fast enough.

"Sobaka!"

"Oh no!" said JR. He knew that word.

"What does that mean?" asked Hazan.

"It means we're in trouble. Run!"

"Okay!" Hazan replied, and before JR could stop her, she'd bolted out in front.

"Wait!" he yelled after her. "Stay with us!"

But Hazan was already several strides ahead. Behind them, humans were shouting.

"Follow her!" JR yelled, and they took off after Hazan.

"Where's she going?" Beatrix gasped.

"I think we're headed for the stage!" shouted Robert.

"Swing right!" JR called back, taking a sharp right into a room packed with humans dressed in rags and holding the leashes of dirty dogs. They were backstage, separated from the crowd by only a curtain. The music was so loud it hurt JR's ears. He scanned the room for Hazan.

He spotted her near the curtain, standing next to a big brown dog. A big brown dog with matted fur and a scar over his right eye—

"Boris!" JR was at his side in a second. The model holding his leash was looking around, confused.

"Boris! You're alive!" Beatrix bounded right up to him and licked his dirty face. "But you're muzzled! Does it hurt?"

Boris looked at them all, dazed. "What? Where—" he began.

"*Sobaka!*"

They all turned to see the short, stout man stomping up to them, muzzles in hand.

"Crikey," said Robert.

"What do we do?" Hazan squeaked.

The model holding Boris's leash gave it a yank, pulling him through the curtain. As it parted, JR caught a glimpse of the stage on the other side, and the crowd beyond. And it gave him a crazy idea.

"Showtime!" he yelled, dashing through the curtain just before the man could reach them. The others followed, stumbling out into the bright lights and leaving the man on the other side of the curtain, cursing.

Onstage, models strutted this way and that, showing off their tattered clothes. A few exchanged uncertain looks when the dogs burst out, then tried to concentrate on their routine. The audience oohed and clapped, unaware that the new dogs weren't officially part of the act.

"What now?" Arne whispered.

JR glanced back at the curtain. Their pursuer was poking his head through, glaring at them. "I guess we strut our stuff?"

Beatrix's face lit up. "Follow me, everyone! I did a kibble commercial when I was a puppy. Keep your heads high and steps light." And she trotted out onto centre stage, turning this way and that so everyone could admire her fur. Diego and Arne shrugged and followed, nodding at the audience. Hazan pranced behind. Robert and JR hung back in the shadows, not wanting John and George to spot them.

"Looks like the catwalk has become a dog-walk," Robert quipped.

JR was about to respond when he noticed the pen in the middle of the stage. The pen where the dog fight—beauty vs. filth, purebred vs. stray—would take place. The pen, he suddenly realized, where he himself would have had to fight if Katerina had had her way. He shivered from his nose to his toenails.

The audience began to clap as the curtain parted again and a new human and dog stepped out. JR turned. It was Katerina, dressed head to toe in black garbage bags. She was holding Pie's leash.

"Pie!" Robert bounded toward his brother, then stopped when Pie walked past without even looking at him. "What the ...?"

Pie strutted down the dogwalk, paused to glare at the audience, then turned back. The crowd cheered.

"Hey," JR said. "He's ... he's *good*." Pie lifted his head as if he were too good for the crowd—as if the human on the end of his leash was a queen and not a bag lady. "He's ... *really* good!"

"And she's really scary!" said Robert.

Katerina struck a pose to show off her garbage bags, but the audience had eyes only for Pie. She frowned and struck another pose.

"Do you think John'll recognize him?" JR whispered.

"I don't know," Robert whispered back. "He's not acting like himself at all."

They watched as Pie tossed his head and gave the audience another smouldering look. The audience's cheers turned to oohs as the curtain parted once again and the angry grey dog lunged out, dragging a model behind him.

Katerina was only too happy to yank Pie toward the pen. The grey dog's model produced a stick and prodded him toward it, too.

"Oh no!" Robert gasped.

Pie froze at the sight of the snarling grey dog, and in an instant, the new, confident Pie had disappeared and the Pie they knew and loved flattened himself on the floor like one of Katerina's paper-thin pancakes.

"Pie!" Robert cried. "Get up! He'll tear you to shreds!"

Katerina leaned over to unfasten Pie's muzzle, a nasty smile spreading across her face.

But just then, a human in the audience stood up. "Pie?" he hollered. *"Pie!"*

Onstage, Pie dared to peek up from the floor.

"Pie!" John Cowley shouted again, shoving his way up to the edge of the stage. "That's my dog! That's Pie!"

Pie leaped to his feet, trembling all over. He squealed at the sight of his human, then bounded across the stage, yanking his leash out of Katerina's hand. When he reached the edge, he didn't even stop, but leaped right off into John's arms.

The crowd went wild. Suddenly, everyone was on their feet, cheering and jostling for a good look at the infuriated Australian and the dog licking his face through a muzzle.

"Who did this?" John bellowed. "Whoever did this will pay for it!"

"Look." Robert nudged JR, pointing with his snout to the side of the stage, where a skinny man in sunglasses and a hat was making a run for the door. "I bet that's Filipov. Let's get him!"

"Wait," said JR. "Not yet. First we have to free the strays."

He called for the other embassy dogs, and together they abandoned the stage and ran back through the curtain. Boris and his model had returned backstage as well; a man was carefully arranging the model's rags while an artist retouched her makeup.

"Give him up, princess!" Beatrix shrieked, barrelling toward the model. She ran straight into her knobby knees, knocking her clean off her feet. "Come on, Boris!"

Boris didn't have to be told twice. With a howl of joy, he joined the embassy dogs in a sprint for the door. Out in the hallway, they retraced their steps back to the room where JR had first seen Pie.

Sergei was still there, standing patiently as the makeup artist drew white stripes on his ears. He jumped when they all burst in, and the artist screamed. Hazan and Diego took care of her, chasing her in circles around the room, then out the door.

"Where are the others?" JR asked Boris. "Can you take us to them?"

Boris nodded. "But they're locked up in cages. Far-too-small cages, I might add."

"Why those horrible old—" Beatrix began.

"Stand still," Arne told Boris, going to work on his muzzle. Within moments, the clasp came open and the muzzle clattered to the floor.

Robert grinned. "I don't think we need to worry about the locks. Let's go!"

Five minutes later, they were in a large room slowly filling up with stray dogs freed from their cages for the first time in days. And all thanks to Arne, who was running from one cage to another, springing open the locks with his teeth.

At that point, Ania burst through the door, followed by all the other metro dogs. Her mouth fell open.

"Ania!" Boris cried.

"Boris!" She leaped over and licked his face. "You're alive!"

"All thanks to our embassy dogs," said Boris.

Ania spun around until she found JR. "Embassy! You did it!" she cried. "Thank you!"

JR's chest swelled with pride, but he shook his head. "I didn't do it," he said, looking around at the other embassy dogs. "We all did."

"*La unión hace la fuerza,*" Diego said.

"Strength in numbers," Arne translated, freeing the last stray from her cage.

Then the big grey dog dashed in, his eyes wild and mouth frothing. Everyone gasped and took a few steps back, and the grey dog stopped to catch his breath.

For a moment, everyone was silent. Then the grey dog let out a whimper. A mournful, submissive, positively Pie-like whimper. "Please," he said, "let me out, too."

Arne hesitated, then jumped up, sprang open his muzzle in record time, and retreated quickly.

The grey dog shook his head, followed by his entire body. Then he let out a huge sigh.

"Is it over?" he asked in barely more than a whisper.

"Not yet," said JR. "We've still got to get out of here."

Someone yelped, and everyone turned to see a skinny man in sunglasses and a black hat standing in the doorway. His mouth hung wide open.

JR stared at the man. Could it be? He sniffed the air, catching a familiar, overpowering whiff of onions and paint thinner.

It was the man with the stuffed potato! *Filipov* had tried to nab JR on his first night out!

For a moment, the dogs just looked at him. Then, one of them began to growl. Another joined in, and another, until the entire room was rumbling.

Filipov gulped and stepped back, murmuring something that JR guessed meant "Good doggies … nice doggies …"

"Get him!" JR yelled, and the dogs surged forward. Filipov ran, and the dogs followed, barking and howling and snapping at his heels.

They chased him out into the night, where a big black car was waiting for him, its back door open. Filipov dove inside and slammed the door just as a dozen dogs threw themselves up against it, scratching the paint and slobbering on the windows. Some even chased it down the street when it drove off.

"I'd say our work here is done," Robert proclaimed, watching them go.

"But he's getting away!" said Beatrix.

"He won't get far," Robert said knowingly. "Not if John has anything to do with it."

Soon, the humans began spilling out of the warehouse.

"Where to now?" someone yelled.

"To the metro!" cried Ania, and everyone howled in agreement. They turned and ran off, shoulder to shoulder, strays and purebreds blending together under the street lights until it was impossible to tell any of them apart.

19

A Country Drive

"Boy, have I got a treat for you."

JR opened one eye to see George tromping into the living room, holding a set of keys in his hand. He blinked and yawned, stretching in the sunbeam that had made for the ideal Saturday morning nap. George had left very early without saying where he was going. It wasn't normal George behaviour, but then, he'd been out of sorts since he'd stopped seeing Katerina.

"We're going for a drive in the country," George announced, jingling the keys. "I rented us a car for the day."

JR sat up. A car ride! In the country! That was even better than a Saturday sunbeam. He was waiting at the door in five seconds flat.

George laughed, opening the door. "I thought you'd like that."

As they cruised down the street in their little green rental car, they passed John Cowley, out walking Robert and Pie. George tooted the horn and waved, and JR put both paws on the window so the shepherds could see him, too.

"Lucky dog!" Robert called out, and Pie laughed. George honked again and drove on. JR settled down in the middle of the back seat for the best view.

"Seems like John's been spending more time with the dogs lately," George commented, fiddling with the radio dial.

JR agreed. He knew all about it. In the month that had passed since the Filipov show, Robert and Pie's lives had changed, and for the better. John no longer headed back to work after dinner every night. Now he took the brothers for long, rambling walks along the river or stayed home and read with them curled at his feet. According to Robert, Pie hadn't destroyed a single thing since he'd returned home.

Pie had changed in other ways, too. He was still shy and submissive, but he didn't flinch at every leaf that blew by him now. And one afternoon at the park, he'd confided in JR that although he was relieved to be back at home, sometimes he wished he'd had more time onstage. Apparently, he was preparing a one-act play based on his experience, and he planned to unveil it someday soon.

George found a radio station playing something upbeat, with lots of drums. He turned it up and started tapping on the steering wheel.

George had never actually found out that Katerina had tried to dognap JR and force him to fight angry strays. Apparently, when he'd come home from work that day, he'd discovered a note from her saying that they were out for a walk and instructing him to head to the show, where she'd meet him later. And by the time he'd returned late that night, head spinning from all he'd seen, JR had been curled up in bed, looking as innocent as a dog who'd just rescued several dozen strays from a famous artist possibly could.

George had crouched down beside him and laid a soft hand on top of his head.

"You'd never guess what happened tonight, boy," he'd said, shaking his head. "You know Cupcake, the Aussie dog who was stolen? Turns out *Filip Filipov* stole him! We saw him in the show, with a whole bunch of other stolen dogs. Can you believe it? I never trusted that guy."

JR had tried hard to look shocked.

"And apparently, he was going to make poor Cupcake fight a stray dog! A mean, slobbery one, by the looks of it. That was the whole 'Beauty vs. Filth' angle. They say it's a statement on society, but I think it's just wrong. Thankfully, the police found him—John made sure of *that*. His lawyers won't let Filipov off easy."

JR snuggled down into his bed and flipped on his side so George could rub his belly.

"But you know what's funny?" George continued. "When I was leaving, someone told me that a huge stack of Filipov's photos, which were somewhere in the warehouse, had been ruined. They were worth hundreds of thousands of dollars. And you know *how*?" George paused, as if expecting JR to guess.

JR waited.

"Apparently, some dog did its *business* on them! Like it was actually trying to get revenge!"

JR tried to suppress a chuckle. He didn't know for sure, but he suspected Fyodor was behind that one.

"So ... I think we've seen the end of Katerina, boy," George continued, sitting cross-legged on the floor. "Turns out she worked for Filipov, so she must have known about the dognapping. John'll probably charge her, too." He shook his head. "I can't believe I was dating a dognapper's assistant. What ... what if she'd tried to take *you*? Where would I be without you, boy?"

JR nuzzled his hand. Despite the smelly cologne and badger-hair shaving brush and the fear of heights and spiders and putting his head underwater, George was a pretty good human.

"Also, she was wearing all this dark makeup at the show. And garbage bags for clothes," George added. "It was kind of scary."

JR nodded. George really had no idea.

George stood up and stretched. "I'm going to take a break from dating for a while, boy. I think I just need some time alone."

JR yawned and rolled his eyes. He'd believe that when he saw it.

Now he watched the red-brick wall of the Kremlin whiz by the window, and he sighed with contentment. Somehow, everything had turned out. All the metro dogs were reunited—slightly thinner than before, since Filipov had been stingy with the kibble, but all in all, none the worse for wear.

JR moved to the window and pressed his nose against it, hoping to catch a glimpse of Ania or Boris or Fyodor. Since George no longer had anywhere to go in the evenings, JR hadn't been able to sneak out and visit them much, and he missed them. Fyodor had promised that next time they went out, he'd show JR a new food acquisition skill called the Fake-an-Injury. He couldn't wait.

Eventually, they ran into a typical Moscow traffic jam, so JR lay down for a nap. When he awoke,

George was veering off the highway onto a nice, quiet road lined with little weathered cottages.

They drove on, passing farms and fields and little glades of birch trees, and JR was just starting to fall asleep again when George shifted gears and slowed.

"Hmm," he said, leaning forward on the steering wheel. "Look over here, boy. It's a *dacha* for sale. Remember Katerina's *dacha*? Apparently they're a big part of Russian culture."

JR sat up and moved to the window. A driveway lined with birch trees wound its way up to a small red-brick house with a moss-green roof. It had a nice grassy yard, and flowers were just beginning to pop up in the garden out front. JR sighed. Now *that* was a home.

"Let's just go take a look," George suggested. "Just to see what the *dacha* fuss is all about."

JR leaped out the back door as soon as George opened it, running up the driveway toward the garden, which probably contained several dozen small, squeaky things.

"Hey, wait!" George called. "Your leash!" Then he looked around. "Oh well, you're probably all right out here. Wow, you sure like this place, don't you, boy?"

JR's back legs did their off-leash dance as he bounded across the grass. He'd just found a pile of feathers that needed inspecting when the *dacha*'s front door opened and a young woman with short brown hair stepped out.

"*Dobryj den,*" she said.

"Oh! *Dobryj den,*" said George. "Um, do you speak English?"

The woman nodded. "Are you here to look at the house?"

George nodded, then shook his head. "Well, we—that is, my dog and I—were just passing by and thought it looked interesting. Is it yours?"

"No." The woman walked down the steps toward George. "I'm the real estate agent. Nadya Komarovski." She held out her hand for George to shake, and he did, eagerly. Nadya was very pretty.

"So you are in the market for a *dacha*?" Nadya asked.

George shook his head. "Oh no. But we're new to Moscow, and we've heard a lot about *dachas.* So lots of Muscovites have them?"

Nadya smiled. "The *dacha* is a wonderful thing—the perfect way to escape the rush and traffic of the city." She looked around the yard, shielding her eyes from the sun. "Whoever buys this one will have very peaceful weekends. There's even a duck pond out back."

JR's ears swivelled. Duck pond? This place *was* a paradise. He imagined the embassy dogs coming out to visit him here. What a time they'd have!

He abandoned the feathers and trotted over to Nadya's feet. She crouched down and scratched his ears, finding the sweet spot right away.

George was turning in a slow circle. "It sure is nice," he said, squinting up at the trees. "Whoever buys it'll be very lucky."

Nadya smiled again. "Maybe it will be you."

JR looked from her to George. He liked Nadya already.

George laughed. "Right. I'll think about it."

Nadya gave JR one last pat and stood up. "Good," she said. "I'll give you my card." She reached into her pocket and handed George her business card.

"Thanks," he said, looking like she'd just handed him a new Dumont-Sauvage Seafaring Nomad AC III. JR rolled his eyes. He'd known George's break from dating would never last.

"So, you're new to Moscow," said Nadya. "Do you think you'll stay?"

JR looked up at George, and George looked down at him, then over at the garden and up at the leafy trees. For a while, he didn't answer, as if thinking hard. JR chewed his lip, knowing that thinking could take George a long time.

Finally, George looked back at Nadya, and gave her a big smile.

"I think we just might."

Acknowledgements

As always, I'm so grateful to so many. First, enormous thanks to my mom, who came with me to Moscow, enduring frostbite on a windswept Kremlin, many hours hopelessly lost on the metro, and an afternoon at the circus (which is another story entirely).

Thanks to my wonderful writing group, the Inkslingers, and to Lynne Missen and Marie Campbell, who loved the idea of the metro dogs from the very beginning. To Karen Alliston for her keen eye and the entire team at Penguin Canada for a warm welcome.

And finally, to the intrepid Masha Rogozhina, who gave us the Grand Tour.

Spasibo to all.